6. On Purim we are required to send two ready-to-eat foods to at least one friend. This is called *Mishloach Manos*. We are also required to give presents to at least two poor people. This is called *Matanos L'Evyonim*.

Did You Know??

Both men and women are required to give *Mishloach Manos* and *Matanos L'Evyonim*. Our Sages teach us that it is more important to give charity to poor people on Purim than to give a very fancy *Mishloach Manos*.

7. We celebrate Purim by being happy, eating, and drinking wine.

Did You Know??

During the day of Purim we have a *Seudas Purim* — a special Purim meal.

A Closer Look

One of the customs of Purim is getting dressed up in a costume. One reason for this is to remember how Hashem "hid Himself" in the Purim story.

ArtScroll Youth Series®

Rabbi Nosson Scherman / Rabbi Meir Zlotowitz

General Editors

מְגִלַּת אֶסְתֵּר
Megillah

Published by

Mesorah Publications, ltd

The ArtScroll
Children's

by **Shmuel Blitz**

Illustrated by Tova Katz

Introduction by
Rabbi Nosson Scherman

The author dedicates this book to
his mother-in-law and her husband
Helen and Harry Gubits

RTSCROLL YOUTH SERIES®

Published by **MESORAH PUBLICATIONS, LTD.**
4401 Second Avenue / Brooklyn, N.Y 11232 / (718) 921-9000 / Fax: (718) 680-1875
e-mail: artscroll@mesorah.com

Distributed in Israel by SIFRIATI / A. GITLER — BOOKS
6 Hayarkon Street / Bnei Brak 51127

Distributed in Europe by LEHMANNS
Unit E, Viking Industrial Park, Rolling Mill Road / Jarrow, Tyne and Wear / England NE32 3DP

Distributed in Australia and New Zealand by GOLD'S WORLD OF JUDAICA
3-13 William Street / Balaclava, Melbourne 3183, Victoria, Australia

Distributed in South Africa by KOLLEL BOOKSHOP
Ivy Common / 105 William Road, Norwood 2192, Johannesburg, South Africa

Printed in the United States of America by Noble Book Press Corp.
Custom bound by Sefercraft, Inc. / 4401 Second Avenue / Brooklyn N.Y. 11232

ISBN 10: 1-57819-708-2 / ISBN 13: 978-1-57819-708-8   (h/c)
ISBN 10: 1-57819-709-0 / ISBN 13: 978-1-57819-709-5   (p/b)

Table of Contents

Introduction

The miracle of Purim took place at a time when the Jewish people didn't expect miracles to happen. In fact, you can read the story of the Megillah and think that it was not a miracle at all. The story doesn't even say that Hashem did anything. Why not?

The story of Purim happened after King Nevuchadnetzar destroyed the Bais HaMikdash. That happened fifty-four years before Achashveirosh became king. Most of the Jews living in the time of Mordechai and Esther were born after the destruction. Many Jews thought that Hashem did not care about them anymore.

Three years after Achashveirosh became king, he became sure that Hashem would never bring the Jews back to Eretz Yisrael. He was so happy that he made a great feast for everyone in his very big kingdom. Mordechai didn't want the Jews to go to the feast. The Jews did not listen to Mordechai because they were afraid the king would be angry if they stayed away. They did not think that Hashem would make a miracle to save them if Achashveirosh wanted to punish them.

What would we have done if we were there? Wouldn't we have been afraid also?

When Esther became the new queen, she and her uncle Mordechai were very sad. Why would a tzadekes like Esther want to be married to a man like Achashveirosh?

Then Haman became the most important person in the whole empire, and everyone had to bow to him. But Mordechai refused to bow. Haman became so angry that he decided to kill all the Jews — and the king told him that was a great idea.

Whose fault was that? Wasn't it Mordechai's fault for making Haman angry? We can imagine that many Jews must have been very angry at Mordechai. First he told them not to go to the king's feast, and now he was giving Haman an excuse to kill them all!

Then things began to happen — very fast. Esther went to the king to try to save her people. Haman wanted to hang Mordechai. The king was reminded that Mordechai had saved his life. Haman was forced to honor Mordechai. Esther turned the king against Haman — and that terrible man was hanged on the same gallows he made for Mordechai. All of this happened in just a few days.

In the end, not only were the Jews saved, but Haman and all their enemies were killed. The Jews used to think that Mordechai was the one who caused them trouble. Now they saw that Mordechai and Esther were the ones who saved them.

The Jews also saw something else. They used to think that Hashem was not around unless He showed us big miracles. Now they saw that Hashem makes things happen even if we don't see Him doing it. They understood that everything that happened in the Megillah story was done by Hashem.

We should thank Haman. He had complained that the Jews have too many holidays — but because of him, we have Purim, our happiest holiday.

Achashveirosh was ready to do everything Esther wanted — except to let the Jews build the Bais HaMikdash. In fact, when he became king, he gave an order that they should stop building it! But when he died, the new king, Daryavesh (Darius), was Esther's son. Daryavesh gave the Jews permission to go back to Jerusalem and build the Second Bais HaMikdash.

Hashem showed that He always helps the Jewish people, even when we don't see His hand.

Rabbi Nosson Scherman

ברכות לפני קריאת המגילה
Blessings Before Reading the Megillah

Before reading *Megillas Esther* on Purim [both at night and again in the morning], the reader recites the following three blessings. The congregation should answer *Amen* only [not בָּרוּךְ הוּא וּבָרוּךְ שְׁמוֹ] after each blessing, and have in mind that they thereby fulfill the obligation of reciting the blessings themselves. During the morning reading, they should also have in mind that the third blessing applies to the other mitzvos of Purim — *shalach manos,* gifts to the poor, and the festive Purim meal — as well as to the *Megillah* reading.

[These blessings are recited whether or not a *minyan* is present for the reading.]

Blessed are You, HASHEM, our God, King of the universe, Who has made us holy with His commandments and has commanded us about the reading of the Megillah.

(Cong. — Amen.)

בָּרוּךְ אַתָּה יהוה אֱלֹהֵינוּ מֶלֶךְ הָעוֹלָם, אֲשֶׁר קִדְּשָׁנוּ בְּמִצְוֹתָיו, וְצִוָּנוּ עַל מִקְרָא מְגִלָּה. (קהל – אָמֵן.)

Blessed are You, HASHEM, our God, King of the universe, Who has made miracles for our forefathers, in those days at this season.

(Cong. — Amen.)

בָּרוּךְ אַתָּה יהוה אֱלֹהֵינוּ מֶלֶךְ הָעוֹלָם, שֶׁעָשָׂה נִסִּים לַאֲבוֹתֵינוּ, בַּיָּמִים הָהֵם, בַּזְּמַן הַזֶּה. (קהל – אָמֵן.)

Blessed are You, HASHEM, our God, King of the universe, Who has kept us alive, preserved us and brought us to this season. (Cong. — Amen.)

בָּרוּךְ אַתָּה יהוה אֱלֹהֵינוּ מֶלֶךְ הָעוֹלָם, שֶׁהֶחֱיָנוּ, וְקִיְּמָנוּ, וְהִגִּיעָנוּ לַזְּמַן הַזֶּה. (קהל – אָמֵן.)

[The Megillah is read.]

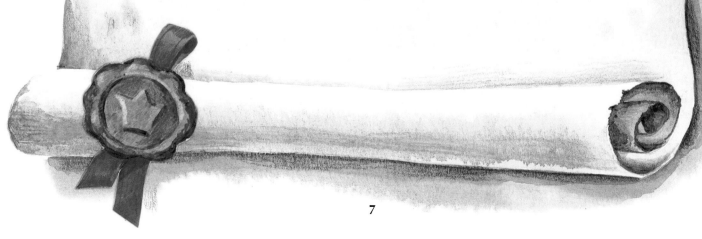

Chapter One — פרק א

אוַיְהִי בִּימֵי אֲחַשְׁוֵרוֹשׁ הוּא אֲחַשְׁוֵרוֹשׁ
הַמֹּלֵךְ מֵהֹדּוּ וְעַד־כּוּשׁ שֶׁבַע וְעֶשְׂרִים
וּמֵאָה מְדִינָה: בּבַּיָּמִים הָהֵם כְּשֶׁבֶת |
הַמֶּלֶךְ אֲחַשְׁוֵרוֹשׁ עַל כִּסֵּא מַלְכוּתוֹ
אֲשֶׁר בְּשׁוּשַׁן הַבִּירָה: גּבִּשְׁנַת שָׁלוֹשׁ
לְמָלְכוֹ עָשָׂה מִשְׁתֶּה לְכָל־שָׂרָיו וַעֲבָדָיו
חֵיל | פָּרַס וּמָדַי הַפַּרְתְּמִים וְשָׂרֵי
הַמְּדִינוֹת לְפָנָיו: דּבְּהַרְאֹתוֹ אֶת־עֹשֶׁר
כְּבוֹד מַלְכוּתוֹ וְאֶת־יְקָר תִּפְאֶרֶת גְּדוּלָּתוֹ
יָמִים רַבִּים שְׁמוֹנִים וּמְאַת יוֹם:

¹ **A**nd it happened during the days of Achashveirosh, who ruled over one hundred twenty-seven countries, from Hodu to Cush.

² King Achashveirosh sat on his royal throne in Shushan the capital.

³ In the third year of his rule, the king made a party for all his officers and servants. The army of Persia and Media, all the noblemen and the officers of the countries were there.

⁴ For one hundred and eighty days, the king showed off his treasures and the greatness of his kingdom.

A Closer Look

Whenever the Bible starts with the words, "וַיְהִי בִּימֵי — And it happened during the days," as it does here, it is telling us that something bad is going to happen.

Did You Know??

The display at this party showed off all the king's wealth. The party lasted for six whole months. Each month had a different theme, meant to show how rich and powerful Achashveirosh was.

A Closer Look

Nebuchadnezzar, the king of Babylonia, destroyed the First *Beis HaMikdash* in Jerusalem. He exiled the Jews to Babylonia. Fifty-one years later, the armies of Persia and Media conquered the Babylonians. Shushan was the capital city of the Persian Empire, and that is where Achashveirosh was king.

Did You Know??

All the gold and silver that Nebuchadnezzar stole from the *Beis HaMikdash* was shown off at the party.

Achashveirosh, the king of Persia, ruled over 127 countries from Hodu to Cush. Some translate these countries as India and Ethiopia.

5 When the party was over, the king made another special party just for the people in Shushan, big and small. This second party lasted for seven days, and it took place in the garden of the king's palace.

6 There were drapes of fine white cotton with blue wool, held in place with fine linen and purple wool, on silver rods and marble columns. There were gold and silver couches, and the floor was made of colorful precious stone.

7 The drinks were served in golden cups. No two cups were the same. There was a great amount of wine — an amount that only a king could provide.

8 The drinks were served with the following rule: "No one is forced to drink." This was done so that each person at the party would be free to do whatever he wanted.

ה וּבִמְלוֹאת ׀ הַיָּמִים הָאֵלֶּה עָשָׂה הַמֶּלֶךְ לְכָל־הָעָם הַנִּמְצְאִים בְּשׁוּשַׁן הַבִּירָה לְמִגָּדוֹל וְעַד־קָטָן מִשְׁתֶּה שִׁבְעַת יָמִים בַּחֲצַר גִּנַּת בִּיתַן הַמֶּלֶךְ: ו חוּר ׀ כַּרְפַּס וּתְכֵלֶת אָחוּז בְּחַבְלֵי־בוּץ וְאַרְגָּמָן עַל־גְּלִילֵי כֶסֶף וְעַמּוּדֵי שֵׁשׁ מִטּוֹת ׀ זָהָב וָכֶסֶף עַל רִצְפַת בַּהַט־וָשֵׁשׁ וְדַר וְסֹחָרֶת: ז וְהַשְׁקוֹת בִּכְלֵי זָהָב וְכֵלִים מִכֵּלִים שׁוֹנִים וְיַיִן מַלְכוּת רָב כְּיַד הַמֶּלֶךְ: ח וְהַשְּׁתִיָּה כַדָּת אֵין אֹנֵס כִּי־כֵן ׀ יִסַּד הַמֶּלֶךְ עַל כָּל־רַב בֵּיתוֹ לַעֲשׂוֹת כִּרְצוֹן אִישׁ־וָאִישׁ:

A Closer Look

After the six-month party was over, everyone in Shushan, including the Jews, were invited to a special seven-day celebration. Achashveirosh and Haman planned this second party in order to make the Jews sin. They hoped the Jews would eat the nonkosher food, violate the Shabbos, and do bad things. This would make Hashem angry at the Jewish people, and then Haman and Achashveirosh would be able to kill all the Jews.

Hashem became angry at the Jewish people for enjoying this seven-day feast. Their leader, Mordechai, had told them not to go, but they didn't listen to him. Hashem also became angry at Achashveirosh for using the holy vessels of the *Beis HaMikdash*.

9 Queen Vashti made a separate party for the women in King Achashverosh's palace.

10 On the seventh day, (the last day of the party), the king was a little drunk. He spoke to his seven main servants — Mehuman, Bizesa, Charvona, Bigesa, Abagesa, Zeisar, and Carcas.

11 The king told them to bring Queen Vashti wearing her royal crown, so the nations and the officers can see how beautiful she is.

ט גַּם וַשְׁתִּי הַמַּלְכָּה עָשְׂתָה מִשְׁתֵּה נָשִׁים בֵּית הַמַּלְכוּת אֲשֶׁר לַמֶּלֶךְ אֲחַשְׁוֵרוֹשׁ:

י בַּיּוֹם הַשְּׁבִיעִי כְּטוֹב לֵב־הַמֶּלֶךְ בַּיָּיִן אָמַר לִמְהוּמָן בִּזְּתָא חַרְבוֹנָא בִּגְתָא וַאֲבַגְתָא זֵתַר וְכַרְכַּס שִׁבְעַת הַסָּרִיסִים הַמְשָׁרְתִים אֶת־פְּנֵי הַמֶּלֶךְ אֲחַשְׁוֵרוֹשׁ:

יא לְהָבִיא אֶת־וַשְׁתִּי הַמַּלְכָּה לִפְנֵי הַמֶּלֶךְ בְּכֶתֶר מַלְכוּת לְהַרְאוֹת הָעַמִּים וְהַשָּׂרִים אֶת־יָפְיָהּ כִּי־טוֹבַת מַרְאֶה הִיא:

Did You Know??

Vashti was the daughter of the Babylonian king Belshazzar and the great-granddaughter of Nebuchadnezzar, who had destroyed the *Beis HaMikdash* and exiled the Jews from Eretz Yisrael.

Vashti was from a family of kings. The women's party would bring her honor.

A Closer Look

The seventh day of this feast was Shabbos.

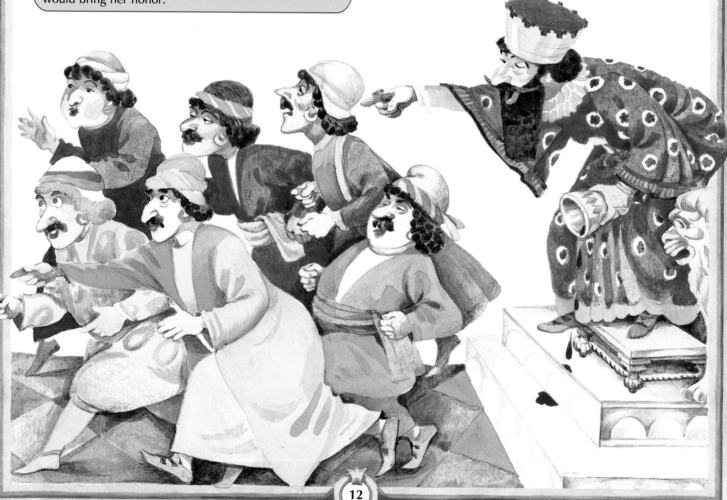

¹² But Queen Vashti refused to listen to the command the king sent with his servants. The king became furious, and he burned with anger.

¹³ Then the king spoke to the wise men. He discussed things with those who knew the laws and rules.

¹⁴ The wise men who were close to the king were Carshena, Shesar, Admasa, Tarshish, Meres, Marsena, and Memuchan. These were the seven officers who were always allowed to see the king; they were the most important people in the land.

יב וַתְּמָאֵ֞ן הַמַּלְכָּ֣ה וַשְׁתִּ֗י לָבוֹא֙ בִּדְבַ֣ר הַמֶּ֔לֶךְ אֲשֶׁ֖ר בְּיַ֣ד הַסָּרִיסִ֑ים וַיִּקְצֹ֤ף הַמֶּ֙לֶךְ֙ מְאֹ֔ד וַחֲמָת֖וֹ בָּעֲרָ֥ה בֽוֹ: יג וַיֹּ֣אמֶר הַמֶּ֔לֶךְ לַחֲכָמִ֖ים יֹדְעֵ֣י הָֽעִתִּ֑ים כִּי־כֵן֙ דְּבַ֣ר הַמֶּ֔לֶךְ לִפְנֵ֕י כָּל־יֹדְעֵ֖י דָּ֥ת וָדִֽין: יד וְהַקָּרֹ֣ב אֵלָ֗יו כַּרְשְׁנָ֤א שֵׁתָר֙ אַדְמָ֣תָא תַרְשִׁ֔ישׁ מֶ֥רֶס מַרְסְנָ֖א מְמוּכָ֑ן שִׁבְעַ֞ת שָׂרֵ֣י ׀ פָּרַ֣ס וּמָדַ֗י רֹאֵי֙ פְּנֵ֣י הַמֶּ֔לֶךְ הַיֹּשְׁבִ֥ים רִאשֹׁנָ֖ה בַּמַּלְכֽוּת:

A Closer Look

Vashti did not want to go to the king because her father was a king. She thought she was much greater than Achashveirosh. Hashem made her grow a tail and her body became full of sores. "I cannot let anyone see me like this," she thought. She did not go to see the king.

Did You Know??

Vashti was evil. Hashem punished her because she forced Jewish girls to work for her on Shabbos. Also, she helped convince the king not to let the Jews rebuild the *Beis HaMikdash* and she used its holy vessels at her party.

15 The king wanted his advisers to tell him how to punish Queen Vashti for not listening to the command the king sent with his servants.

16 Memuchan spoke up first to the king and to his officers. "Queen Vashti has done something wrong not just to the king, but to all his officers and to all the people in every nation that Achashveirosh rules.

17 "All the women will find out what the queen did and they will not respect or listen to their husbands. They will say, 'King Achashveirosh ordered Queen Vashti to come, and she did not listen.'

18 "When the princesses of Persia and Media will hear about the queen, they will do the same thing to the king's officers and it will cause much embarrassment and anger.

טו כְּדָת֙ מַֽה־לַּעֲשׂ֔וֹת בַּמַּלְכָּ֖ה וַשְׁתִּ֑י עַ֣ל ׀ אֲשֶׁ֣ר לֹֽא־עָשְׂתָ֗ה אֶֽת־מַאֲמַר֙ הַמֶּ֣לֶךְ אֲחַשְׁוֵר֔וֹשׁ בְּיַ֖ד הַסָּרִיסִֽים: טז וַיֹּ֣אמֶר מְמוּכָ֗ן [°מוּמְכָן כ׳] לִפְנֵ֤י הַמֶּ֨לֶךְ֙ וְהַשָּׂרִ֔ים לֹ֤א עַל־הַמֶּ֨לֶךְ֙ לְבַדּ֔וֹ עָוְתָ֖ה וַשְׁתִּ֣י הַמַּלְכָּ֑ה כִּ֤י עַל־כָּל־הַשָּׂרִים֙ וְעַל־כָּל־הָ֣עַמִּ֔ים אֲשֶׁ֕ר בְּכָל־מְדִינ֖וֹת הַמֶּ֥לֶךְ אֲחַשְׁוֵרֽוֹשׁ: יז כִּֽי־יֵצֵ֤א דְבַר־הַמַּלְכָּה֙ עַל־כָּל־הַנָּשִׁ֔ים לְהַבְז֥וֹת בַּעְלֵיהֶ֖ן בְּעֵֽינֵיהֶ֑ן בְּאָמְרָ֗ם הַמֶּ֨לֶךְ אֲחַשְׁוֵר֜וֹשׁ אָמַ֗ר לְהָבִ֞יא אֶת־וַשְׁתִּ֧י הַמַּלְכָּ֛ה לְפָנָ֖יו וְלֹא־בָֽאָה: יח וְֽהַיּ֨וֹם הַזֶּ֜ה תֹּאמַ֣רְנָה ׀ שָׂר֣וֹת פָּֽרַס־וּמָדַ֗י אֲשֶׁ֤ר שָֽׁמְעוּ֙ אֶת־דְּבַ֣ר הַמַּלְכָּ֔ה לְכֹ֖ל שָׂרֵ֣י הַמֶּ֑לֶךְ וּכְדַ֖י בִּזָּי֥וֹן וָקָֽצֶף:

Did You Know??
Our Sages teach that Memuchan was Haman. He told Achashveirosh, "The people make fun of a king who cannot control his own wife! Also, other women will stop respecting and listening to their husbands." So the king said Vashti should be killed!

Once Achashveirosh was no longer drunk, he did not want Vashti to be killed, but it was too late, because he had already said that she must be killed.

A Closer Look
Vashti was the last royal descendant of Nebuchadnezzar, who destroyed the First *Beis HaMikdash*. Her death was Nebuchadnezzar's final punishment.

Vashti was executed on Shabbos because she forced Jewish girls to work on Shabbos.

14

יט אִם־עַל־הַמֶּלֶךְ טוֹב יֵצֵא דְבַר־מַלְכוּת מִלְּפָנָיו וְיִכָּתֵב בְּדָתֵי פָרַס־וּמָדַי וְלֹא יַעֲבוֹר אֲשֶׁר לֹא־תָבוֹא וַשְׁתִּי לִפְנֵי הַמֶּלֶךְ אֲחַשְׁוֵרוֹשׁ וּמַלְכוּתָהּ יִתֵּן הַמֶּלֶךְ לִרְעוּתָהּ הַטּוֹבָה מִמֶּנָּה: כ וְנִשְׁמַע פִּתְגָם הַמֶּלֶךְ אֲשֶׁר־יַעֲשֶׂה בְּכָל־מַלְכוּתוֹ כִּי רַבָּה הִיא וְכָל־הַנָּשִׁים יִתְּנוּ יְקָר לְבַעְלֵיהֶן לְמִגָּדוֹל וְעַד־קָטָן: כא וַיִּיטַב הַדָּבָר בְּעֵינֵי הַמֶּלֶךְ וְהַשָּׂרִים וַיַּעַשׂ הַמֶּלֶךְ כִּדְבַר מְמוּכָן: כב וַיִּשְׁלַח סְפָרִים אֶל־כָּל־מְדִינוֹת הַמֶּלֶךְ אֶל־מְדִינָה וּמְדִינָה כִּכְתָבָהּ וְאֶל־עַם וָעָם כִּלְשׁוֹנוֹ לִהְיוֹת כָּל־אִישׁ שֹׂרֵר בְּבֵיתוֹ וּמְדַבֵּר כִּלְשׁוֹן עַמּוֹ:

19 "If the king thinks this is a good idea, he should issue a royal law that will be written forever in the law books of Persia and Media. Let Vashti never be allowed to come to King Achashveirosh, and let the king make a new queen, someone who is better than Vashti.

20 "The ruling of what the king will do will be heard throughout the entire great kingdom. Then every wife in the land will honor her husband."

21 The king and his officers liked this idea, and the king did just as Memuchan suggested.

22 Letters were sent out to every country that the king ruled. Each country received the letter in its own language. It said that each man will be the ruler in his own house, and the family should speak his language.

Chapter Two — פרק ב

¹ After all this happened, King Achashveirosh calmed down and was no longer angry. He remembered Vashti, what she had done, and how she had been punished.

² The young servants of the king then said to him, "Let beautiful girls be found for the king.

³ "The king should appoint officers in every country in his kingdom who will gather together all the young pretty girls to Shushan, the capital. They will be put in the harem under the care of Hegai, the king's servant in charge of the women, and they will be given makeup.

א אַחַר הַדְּבָרִים הָאֵלֶּה כְּשֹׁךְ חֲמַת הַמֶּלֶךְ אֲחַשְׁוֵרוֹשׁ זָכַר אֶת־וַשְׁתִּי וְאֵת אֲשֶׁר־עָשָׂתָה וְאֵת אֲשֶׁר־נִגְזַר עָלֶיהָ: ב וַיֹּאמְרוּ נַעֲרֵי־הַמֶּלֶךְ מְשָׁרְתָיו יְבַקְשׁוּ לַמֶּלֶךְ נְעָרוֹת בְּתוּלוֹת טוֹבוֹת מַרְאֶה: ג וְיַפְקֵד הַמֶּלֶךְ פְּקִידִים בְּכָל־מְדִינוֹת מַלְכוּתוֹ וְיִקְבְּצוּ אֶת־כָּל־נַעֲרָה־בְתוּלָה טוֹבַת מַרְאֶה אֶל־שׁוּשַׁן הַבִּירָה אֶל־בֵּית הַנָּשִׁים אֶל־יַד הֵגֶא סְרִיס הַמֶּלֶךְ שֹׁמֵר הַנָּשִׁים וְנָתוֹן תַּמְרֻקֵיהֶן:

A Closer Look
After King Achashveirosh had Vashti killed, he was sorry about what he had done, and was upset at those who had said to kill her.

Did You Know??
There were searches in all 127 provinces that the king ruled. Most of the time people want their daughter to become the queen. But people were afraid of Achashveirosh and they hid their daughters from the officers. The search took four years.

4 "And the girl that the king likes best will become queen and take Vashti's place." The king was happy with this advice, and he did what they said.

וְהַנַּעֲרָה אֲשֶׁר תִּיטַב בְּעֵינֵי הַמֶּלֶךְ תִּמְלֹךְ תַּחַת וַשְׁתִּי וַיִּיטַב הַדָּבָר בְּעֵינֵי הַמֶּלֶךְ וַיַּעַשׂ כֵּן:

THE NEXT VERSE IS READ ALOUD FIRST BY THE CONGREGATION AND THEN BY THE READER.

5 **There was a Jewish man in the capital city of Shushan whose name was Mordechai the son of Yair, the son of Shim'i, the son of Kish. He was from the tribe of Binyamin.**

6 He had been made to leave Jerusalem together with the Jews who left with King Yechaniah. They had been forced to leave by Nebuchadnezzar, the king of Babylon.

7 Mordechai had a cousin named Hadassah, who was also called Esther. He raised her because she did not have a father or mother. She was very beautiful. When her parents died, Mordechai raised her as his own daughter.

ה אִישׁ יְהוּדִי הָיָה בְּשׁוּשַׁן הַבִּירָה וּשְׁמוֹ מָרְדֳּכַי בֶּן יָאִיר בֶּן־שִׁמְעִי בֶּן־קִישׁ אִישׁ יְמִינִי: ו אֲשֶׁר הָגְלָה מִירוּשָׁלַיִם עִם־הַגֹּלָה אֲשֶׁר הָגְלְתָה עִם יְכָנְיָה מֶלֶךְ־יְהוּדָה אֲשֶׁר הֶגְלָה נְבוּכַדְנֶאצַּר מֶלֶךְ בָּבֶל: ז וַיְהִי אֹמֵן אֶת־הֲדַסָּה הִיא אֶסְתֵּר בַּת־דֹּדוֹ כִּי אֵין לָהּ אָב וָאֵם וְהַנַּעֲרָה יְפַת־תֹּאַר וְטוֹבַת מַרְאֶה וּבְמוֹת אָבִיהָ וְאִמָּהּ לְקָחָהּ מָרְדֳּכַי לוֹ לְבַת:

Did You Know??
Mordechai was a member of the Sanhedrin, the High Court of the Jews.

Did You Know??

Esther's father, Avichayil, died before she was born. Her mother died as she was born. Mordechai adopted her when she was a young girl.

Some Sages say that her name was really Esther but that she was called Hadassah because she was like a myrtle twig (*hadas*). A myrtle smells nice but is bitter to eat; Esther was nice to Mordechai, but was bitter for Haman.

Other Sages say that her name was really Hadassah, but she was called Esther because Esther is similar to *hester*, which means "hidden." Her family was hidden from people, since she did not tell them she was Jewish. Every country claimed she was one of theirs.

In most places, Verse 5 is said out loud by everyone, and it is then repeated by the person reading the Megillah. This is done with several verses that show how the Jews were saved. This shows our joy.

⁸ When people heard about the king's command and many young girls were brought to Shushan the capital, under the care of Hegai, Esther was also taken to the palace. She was taken care of by Hegai, the guard of the women.

⁹ Hegai liked Esther and wanted to be good to her. He rushed to make sure she got her cosmetics and her meals, and he brought her seven maids from the palace. He changed the rooms of Esther and her maids to the best rooms in the harem.

¹⁰ Esther told no one what her nation was or about her family, because Mordechai told her not to.

ח וַיְהִ֗י בְּהִשָּׁמַ֤ע דְּבַר־הַמֶּ֙לֶךְ֙ וְדָת֔וֹ וּֽבְהִקָּבֵ֞ץ נְעָר֥וֹת רַבּ֛וֹת אֶל־שׁוּשַׁ֥ן הַבִּירָ֖ה אֶל־יַ֣ד הֵגָ֑י וַתִּלָּקַ֤ח אֶסְתֵּר֙ אֶל־בֵּ֣ית הַמֶּ֔לֶךְ אֶל־יַ֥ד הֵגַ֖י שֹׁמֵ֥ר הַנָּשִֽׁים׃ ט וַתִּיטַ֨ב הַנַּעֲרָ֣ה בְעֵינָיו֘ וַתִּשָּׂ֣א חֶ֣סֶד לְפָנָיו֒ וַ֠יְבַהֵ֠ל אֶת־תַּמְרוּקֶ֤יהָ וְאֶת־מָנוֹתֶ֙יהָ֙ לָתֵ֣ת לָ֔הּ וְאֵת֙ שֶׁ֣בַע הַנְּעָר֔וֹת הָרְאֻי֥וֹת לָֽתֶת־לָ֖הּ מִבֵּ֣ית הַמֶּ֑לֶךְ וַיְשַׁנֶּ֧הָ וְאֶת־נַעֲרוֹתֶ֛יהָ לְט֖וֹב בֵּ֥ית הַנָּשִֽׁים׃ י לֹא־הִגִּ֣ידָה אֶסְתֵּ֔ר אֶת־עַמָּ֖הּ וְאֶת־מֽוֹלַדְתָּ֑הּ כִּ֧י מׇרְדֳּכַ֛י צִוָּ֥ה עָלֶ֖יהָ אֲשֶׁ֥ר לֹא־תַגִּֽיד׃

Did You Know??

Esther used a different maid for each day of the week. This way, she was able to keep track of when it was Shabbos. The maids who saw Esther on weekdays did not realize that she rested on Shabbos. The maid who came only on Shabbos saw Esther resting all day and not doing any work. She assumed that this was what Esther did every day. This way no one suspected that Esther was Jewish.

A Closer Look

Mordechai hid Esther because he did not want her to be taken to the king's palace. When officers told Achashveirosh that Esther was not among the girls, he ordered that any girl found hiding from the officers would be killed.

11 Every day Mordechai walked past the courtyard of the harem to find out how Esther was doing, and to see what was happening to her.

יא וּבְכָל־יוֹם וָיוֹם מָרְדְּכַי מִתְהַלֵּךְ לִפְנֵי חֲצַר בֵּית־הַנָּשִׁים לָדַעַת אֶת־שְׁלוֹם אֶסְתֵּר וּמַה־יֵּעָשֶׂה בָּהּ:

Did You Know??
While at the palace, Esther got special food, so that everything she ate was kosher.

¹² Every girl had her turn to come before King Achashveirosh, after receiving beauty treatments for twelve months. For six months they were treated with oil of myrrh, and for six months they were treated with perfumes and cosmetics.

¹³ The girl was then brought to the king. She was given anything she asked for to take along with her to the king.

¹⁴ She would come in the evening, and in the morning she would be brought to a second harem under the care of Shaashgaz, the king's servant, who guarded the king's wives. The girl was never allowed to go to the king again, unless he called for her by name.

יב וּבְהַגִּיעַ תֹּר נַעֲרָה וְנַעֲרָה לָבוֹא ׀ אֶל־הַמֶּלֶךְ אֲחַשְׁוֵרוֹשׁ מִקֵּץ הֱיוֹת לָהּ כְּדָת הַנָּשִׁים שְׁנֵים עָשָׂר חֹדֶשׁ כִּי כֵּן יִמְלְאוּ יְמֵי מְרוּקֵיהֶן שִׁשָּׁה חֳדָשִׁים בְּשֶׁמֶן הַמֹּר וְשִׁשָּׁה חֳדָשִׁים בַּבְּשָׂמִים וּבְתַמְרוּקֵי הַנָּשִׁים: יג וּבָזֶה הַנַּעֲרָה בָּאָה אֶל־הַמֶּלֶךְ אֵת כָּל־אֲשֶׁר תֹּאמַר יִנָּתֵן לָהּ לָבוֹא עִמָּהּ מִבֵּית הַנָּשִׁים עַד־בֵּית הַמֶּלֶךְ: יד בָּעֶרֶב ׀ הִיא בָאָה וּבַבֹּקֶר הִיא שָׁבָה אֶל־בֵּית הַנָּשִׁים שֵׁנִי אֶל־יַד שַׁעַשְׁגַז סְרִיס הַמֶּלֶךְ שֹׁמֵר הַפִּילַגְשִׁים לֹא־תָבוֹא עוֹד אֶל־הַמֶּלֶךְ כִּי אִם־חָפֵץ בָּהּ הַמֶּלֶךְ וְנִקְרְאָה בְשֵׁם:

A Closer Look

After being taken to the king, these girls were never allowed to marry anyone else, even if the king never wanted to see them again.

20

¹⁵ And when it was the turn of Esther, the daughter of Mordechai's uncle Avichayil, whom Mordechai had adopted as his own daughter, to come before the king, she asked for nothing. She just took what Hegai, the king's servant, told her to take. Whoever saw Esther liked her.

¹⁶ Esther was brought to the palace and taken to Achashveirosh. It was the tenth month, the month of Teves, in the seventh year of the king's rule.

¹⁷ The king loved Esther more than any of the other women. He favored her more than any of the other girls. He placed the royal crown on her head and made her queen instead of Vashti.

טו וּבְהַגִּיעַ תֹּר־אֶסְתֵּר בַּת־אֲבִיחַיִל | דֹּד מָרְדֳּכַי אֲשֶׁר לָקַח־לוֹ לְבַת לָבוֹא אֶל־הַמֶּלֶךְ לֹא בִקְשָׁה דָּבָר כִּי אִם אֶת־אֲשֶׁר יֹאמַר הֵגַי סְרִיס־הַמֶּלֶךְ שֹׁמֵר הַנָּשִׁים וַתְּהִי אֶסְתֵּר נֹשֵׂאת חֵן בְּעֵינֵי כָּל־רֹאֶיהָ: טז וַתִּלָּקַח אֶסְתֵּר אֶל־הַמֶּלֶךְ אֲחַשְׁוֵרוֹשׁ אֶל־בֵּית מַלְכוּתוֹ בַּחֹדֶשׁ הָעֲשִׂירִי הוּא־חֹדֶשׁ טֵבֵת בִּשְׁנַת־שֶׁבַע לְמַלְכוּתוֹ: יז וַיֶּאֱהַב הַמֶּלֶךְ אֶת־אֶסְתֵּר מִכָּל־הַנָּשִׁים וַתִּשָּׂא־חֵן וָחֶסֶד לְפָנָיו מִכָּל־הַבְּתוּלֹת וַיָּשֶׂם כֶּתֶר־מַלְכוּת בְּרֹאשָׁהּ וַיַּמְלִיכֶהָ תַּחַת וַשְׁתִּי:

A Closer Look
Esther did not bring along anything special when she went to the king, because she hoped that Achashveirosh would not like her and would not pick her to be his queen.

21

18 Then the king made a big party for all his officers and all his servants. This was "Esther's Party." The king announced that none of the countries in the kingdom would have to pay taxes, and he gave out gifts that only a king is able to afford.

19 All the girls of the harem were brought together a second time; and Mordechai would sit at the king's gate.

20 Esther did not tell anyone where she was born or who her people were, just as Mordechai had commanded her. Esther did whatever Mordechai said — just as she did when she was growing up with him.

יח וַיַּעַשׂ הַמֶּלֶךְ מִשְׁתֶּה גָדוֹל לְכָל־שָׂרָיו וַעֲבָדָיו אֵת מִשְׁתֵּה אֶסְתֵּר וַהֲנָחָה לַמְּדִינוֹת עָשָׂה וַיִּתֵּן מַשְׂאֵת כְּיַד הַמֶּלֶךְ: יט וּבְהִקָּבֵץ בְּתוּלוֹת שֵׁנִית וּמָרְדֳּכַי יֹשֵׁב בְּשַׁעַר־הַמֶּלֶךְ: כ אֵין אֶסְתֵּר מַגֶּדֶת מוֹלַדְתָּהּ וְאֶת־עַמָּהּ כַּאֲשֶׁר צִוָּה עָלֶיהָ מָרְדֳּכָי וְאֶת־מַאֲמַר מָרְדֳּכַי אֶסְתֵּר עֹשָׂה כַּאֲשֶׁר הָיְתָה בְאָמְנָה אִתּוֹ:

Did You Know??

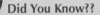

Achashveirosh was trying to find out what nation Esther was from. First he made a giant party, but she did not tell. Then he canceled all taxes in her honor, but she still did not tell him. Then he gave his subjects valuable gifts in her honor, but she would still not tell. The Jews knew that Mordechai had told her not to say where she was from, so not one of them told Achashveirosh or his officers, either.

A Closer Look

Here are some of the reasons why Mordechai did not want anyone to know that Esther was Jewish. 1. If Esther was chosen as queen, it must be that Hashem was using her to save the Jewish people. Achashveirosh would not have chosen her if he had known she was Jewish. 2. If no one knew she was Jewish, it would be easier for her to follow the Torah's commandments. 3. He did not want Achashveirosh to know that she was a great-granddaughter of King Shaul. He hoped Achashveirosh would think she came from a simple background and therefore would not choose her to become queen.

A Closer Look

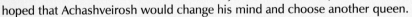

Why were the girls gathered together after Esther was chosen? Achashveirosh was upset that Esther would not tell him what nation she was from. He asked Mordechai for an idea, and Mordechai suggested that he gather the girls, to see if he would pick someone else to be his queen. He told Achashveirosh that this would make Esther jealous and she may tell him where she was from. Actually, Mordechai hoped that Achashveirosh would change his mind and choose another queen.

²¹ In those days, when Mordechai was sitting at the king's gate. Bigsan and Teresh — two of the king's servants who guarded the door-way — got angry. They planned to kill king Achashveirosh.

²² Mordechai found out about this plot and told Esther about it. Esther then told the king, saying she heard about it from Mordechai.

²³ The story was investigated and they found that it was true. Bigsan and Teresh were hanged, and this story was written in the record book of the king.

כא בַּיָּמִים הָהֵם וּמָרְדֳּכַי יֹשֵׁב בְּשַׁעַר־הַמֶּלֶךְ קָצַף בִּגְתָן וָתֶרֶשׁ שְׁנֵי־סָרִיסֵי הַמֶּלֶךְ מִשֹּׁמְרֵי הַסַּף וַיְבַקְשׁוּ לִשְׁלֹחַ יָד בַּמֶּלֶךְ אֲחַשְׁוֵרֹשׁ: כב וַיִּוָּדַע הַדָּבָר לְמָרְדֳּכַי וַיַּגֵּד לְאֶסְתֵּר הַמַּלְכָּה וַתֹּאמֶר אֶסְתֵּר לַמֶּלֶךְ בְּשֵׁם מָרְדֳּכָי: כג וַיְבֻקַּשׁ הַדָּבָר וַיִּמָּצֵא וַיִּתָּלוּ שְׁנֵיהֶם עַל־עֵץ וַיִּכָּתֵב בְּסֵפֶר דִּבְרֵי הַיָּמִים לִפְנֵי הַמֶּלֶךְ:

A Closer Look

Why was Mordechai at the palace gate? Because he felt that these were dangerous times for the Jewish people, and at the king's gate he would hear about any plans against the Jews.

Did You Know??

When Bigsan and Teresh plotted to kill the king, they spoke in the Tarsian language, which they thought no one in Shushan would know. As a member of the Great Sanhedrin, though, Mordechai understood all seventy languages.

Bigsan and Teresh wanted to kill the king by poisoning him.

Chapter Three — פרק ג

¹ After these things happened, King Achashveirosh made Haman the son of Hamedasa, the Agagite, important, and gave him a high position. He made Haman more important than all the other officers.

² All the servants of the king at the royal gate would kneel and bow down to Haman because this is what the king ordered. But Mordechai would not kneel or bow down.

אאַחַ֣ר ׀ הַדְּבָרִ֣ים הָאֵ֗לֶּה גִּדַּל֩ הַמֶּ֨לֶךְ אֲחַשְׁוֵר֜וֹשׁ אֶת־הָמָ֧ן בֶּן־הַמְּדָ֛תָא הָאֲגָגִ֖י וַֽיְנַשְּׂאֵ֑הוּ וַיָּ֨שֶׂם֙ אֶת־כִּסְא֔וֹ מֵעַ֕ל כָּל־הַשָּׂרִ֖ים אֲשֶׁ֥ר אִתּֽוֹ: בוְכָל־עַבְדֵ֨י הַמֶּ֜לֶךְ אֲשֶׁר־בְּשַׁ֣עַר הַמֶּ֗לֶךְ כֹּרְעִ֤ים וּמִֽשְׁתַּֽחֲוִים֙ לְהָמָ֔ן כִּי־כֵ֖ן צִוָּה־ל֣וֹ הַמֶּ֑לֶךְ וּמָ֨רְדֳּכַ֔י לֹ֥א יִכְרַ֖ע וְלֹ֥א יִֽשְׁתַּֽחֲוֶֽה:

A Closer Look
If Haman was so evil, why did Hashem let him succeed and gain so much power? The reason is that his downfall would be much greater if he were an important, prominent person.

Did You Know??
Haman had an idol sewn onto his clothing and he himself claimed to be godly. This is why Mordechai would not bow down to him.

³ The king's servants at the palace gates said to Mordechai, "Why are you not listening to the commandment of the king?"

⁴ After they said this to him day after day but he did not listen to them, they told this to Haman. They wanted to see what would happen, since Mordechai had told them that he was a Jew.

⁵ Haman saw that Mordechai was not kneeling or bowing down to him, and he became very angry.

⁶ Haman decided that it would not be enough to punish just Mordechai, because they told him that Mordechai was a Jew. Haman wanted to destroy all of Mordechai's people everywhere in the kingdom of Achashveirosh.

ג וַיֹּאמְרוּ עַבְדֵי הַמֶּלֶךְ אֲשֶׁר־בְּשַׁעַר הַמֶּלֶךְ לְמָרְדֳּכָי מַדּוּעַ אַתָּה עוֹבֵר אֵת מִצְוַת הַמֶּלֶךְ: ד וַיְהִי °כְּאָמְרָם [ᵏבְּאָמְרָם] אֵלָיו יוֹם וָיוֹם וְלֹא שָׁמַע אֲלֵיהֶם וַיַּגִּידוּ לְהָמָן לִרְאוֹת הֲיַעַמְדוּ דִּבְרֵי מָרְדֳּכַי כִּי־הִגִּיד לָהֶם אֲשֶׁר־הוּא יְהוּדִי: ה וַיַּרְא הָמָן כִּי־אֵין מָרְדֳּכַי כֹּרֵעַ וּמִשְׁתַּחֲוֶה לוֹ וַיִּמָּלֵא הָמָן חֵמָה: ו וַיִּבֶז בְּעֵינָיו לִשְׁלֹחַ יָד בְּמָרְדֳּכַי לְבַדּוֹ כִּי־הִגִּידוּ לוֹ אֶת־עַם מָרְדֳּכָי וַיְבַקֵּשׁ הָמָן לְהַשְׁמִיד אֶת־כָּל־הַיְּהוּדִים אֲשֶׁר בְּכָל־מַלְכוּת אֲחַשְׁוֵרוֹשׁ עַם מָרְדֳּכָי:

Did You Know??

Haman was a descendent of Amalek. After the Exodus from Egypt, Amalek attacked the Jewish people in the desert. Hashem commanded the Jewish people to destroy all of Amalek.

Hundreds of years later, Hashem ordered King Shaul to wipe out the entire nation of Amalek, but Shaul had pity on Agag, the king of Amalek, and let him live. Haman was a descendent of Agag. If King Shaul would have done what he was told, Haman would never have been born. This teaches us that we must listen to all of Hashem's commands, even if we do not understand them. Hashem always knows what is best.

A Closer Look

Haman knew that Mordechai was not bowing because of his religion, so he decided to kill all of the Jewish people.

7 In Nisan, the first month of the year, in the twelfth year of Achashveirosh's rule, Haman made a lottery to see which would be the best day and month to destroy the Jews. The twelfth month of the year, Adar, was picked.

בַּחֹדֶשׁ הָרִאשׁוֹן הוּא־חֹדֶשׁ נִיסָן בִּשְׁנַת שְׁתֵּים עֶשְׂרֵה לַמֶּלֶךְ אֲחַשְׁוֵרוֹשׁ הִפִּיל פּוּר הוּא הַגּוֹרָל לִפְנֵי הָמָן מִיּוֹם ׀ לְיוֹם וּמֵחֹדֶשׁ לְחֹדֶשׁ שְׁנֵים־עָשָׂר הוּא־חֹדֶשׁ אֲדָר:

Did You Know??

Whenever Haman had an important decision to make, he always used a lottery.

Haman thought Adar was an unlucky month for the Jews because that is the month when Moshe Rabbeinu died. He did not realize that Adar is also the month that Moshe was born (he was born and he died on the seventh of Adar).

A Closer Look

Haman would have liked to kill the Jews the very next day. But Hashem arranged the lottery so that the time to kill the Jews would be in Adar, which was a whole year away. This would give them a chance to repent and be saved.

8 Haman said to King Achashveirosh: "There is a nation spread out among all the other nations in every country that you rule. Their laws are different from everyone else's laws, and they do not follow the king's laws. It is not worthwhile for the king to allow them to remain this way.

9 "If it pleases the king, let it be written that they be destroyed. And I will pay, through those who do the work, ten thousand talents of silver into the king's treasury.''

ח וַיֹּאמֶר הָמָן לַמֶּלֶךְ אֲחַשְׁוֵרוֹשׁ יֶשְׁנוֹ עַם־אֶחָד מְפֻזָּר וּמְפֹרָד בֵּין הָעַמִּים בְּכֹל מְדִינוֹת מַלְכוּתֶךָ וְדָתֵיהֶם שֹׁנוֹת מִכָּל־עָם וְאֶת־דָּתֵי הַמֶּלֶךְ אֵינָם עֹשִׂים וְלַמֶּלֶךְ אֵין־שֹׁוֶה לְהַנִּיחָם: ט אִם־עַל־הַמֶּלֶךְ טוֹב יִכָּתֵב לְאַבְּדָם וַעֲשֶׂרֶת אֲלָפִים כִּכַּר־כֶּסֶף אֶשְׁקוֹל עַל־יְדֵי עֹשֵׂי הַמְּלָאכָה לְהָבִיא אֶל־גִּנְזֵי הַמֶּלֶךְ:

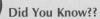

Did You Know??

There has never been a greater slanderer than Haman. He told Achashveirosh, "The Jews make fun of the king. If a fly falls into a Jew's cup of wine, he takes out the fly and drinks the wine. But if the king would even touch a Jew's cup of wine, the Jew would spill it out on the floor."

A Jew may not drink wine touched by a non-Jew, because wine is often used for idol worship. Haman was able to turn around the law to make it seem terrible.

A Closer Look

King Achashveirosh was worried that if the Jews were destroyed he would not be able to collect as much money in taxes. So Haman offered to give him ten thousand silver talents, to make up for lost taxes.

10 The king took his royal ring, the ring with his seal, off his finger, and gave it to Haman the son of Hamedasa, the Agagite, the enemy of the Jewish people.

11 The king said to Haman, "Keep the silver you wanted to give me, and do whatever you want with that nation."

י וַיָּסַר הַמֶּלֶךְ אֶת־טַבַּעְתּוֹ מֵעַל יָדוֹ וַיִּתְּנָהּ לְהָמָן בֶּן־הַמְּדָתָא הָאֲגָגִי צֹרֵר הַיְּהוּדִים: יא וַיֹּאמֶר הַמֶּלֶךְ לְהָמָן הַכֶּסֶף נָתוּן לָךְ וְהָעָם לַעֲשׂוֹת בּוֹ כַּטּוֹב בְּעֵינֶיךָ:

Did You Know??

Once Haman had the ring with the king's seal on it, he was able to write laws.

Ten thousand talents of silver weigh 750 tons — the weight of more than a hundred full-grown elephants.

A Closer Look

King Achashveirosh hated the Jews even more than Haman did. When Haman offered the king ten thousand talents of silver, Achashveirosh told him to keep his money because it would be a big enough favor just to destroy all the Jews.

¹² The king's scribes were called together on the thirteenth day of Nisan, the first month of the year. They wrote everything Haman had ordered. They addressed the letters to each of the rulers in each of the lands, to the officers of every country. The letter to each country was written in that country's own alphabet and language. It was written in the name of King Achashveirosh and stamped with his royal seal.

יב וַיִּקָּרְאוּ סֹפְרֵי הַמֶּלֶךְ בַּחֹדֶשׁ הָרִאשׁוֹן בִּשְׁלוֹשָׁה עָשָׂר יוֹם בּוֹ וַיִּכָּתֵב כְּכָל־אֲשֶׁר־צִוָּה הָמָן אֶל אֲחַשְׁדַּרְפְּנֵי־הַמֶּלֶךְ וְאֶל־הַפַּחוֹת אֲשֶׁר ׀ עַל־מְדִינָה וּמְדִינָה וְאֶל־שָׂרֵי עַם וָעָם מְדִינָה וּמְדִינָה כִּכְתָבָהּ וְעַם וָעָם כִּלְשׁוֹנוֹ בְּשֵׁם הַמֶּלֶךְ אֲחַשְׁוֵרֹשׁ נִכְתָּב וְנֶחְתָּם בְּטַבַּעַת הַמֶּלֶךְ:

29

¹³ Speedy messengers went to every country that the king ruled, bringing letters that said to destroy, to kill, and to wipe out all the Jews, young and old, even children and women. It should be done in one day, on the thirteenth day of the twelfth month, the month of Adar. The people would also be allowed to take all the Jews' property.

יג וְנִשְׁלוֹחַ סְפָרִים בְּיַד הָרָצִים אֶל־כָּל־מְדִינוֹת הַמֶּלֶךְ לְהַשְׁמִיד לַהֲרֹג וּלְאַבֵּד אֶת־כָּל־הַיְּהוּדִים מִנַּעַר וְעַד־זָקֵן טַף וְנָשִׁים בְּיוֹם אֶחָד בִּשְׁלוֹשָׁה עָשָׂר לְחֹדֶשׁ שְׁנֵים־עָשָׂר הוּא־חֹדֶשׁ אֲדָר וּשְׁלָלָם לָבוֹז:

Did You Know??

Haman and Achashveirosh then sat down and drank wine together to celebrate this "Final Solution" to destroy the Jewish people.

When the Jews of Shushan would go into a store to buy something, the owner would laugh and say, "Soon all your money will be mine!"

A Closer Look

Haman was in a big rush to send out this letter, even though the Jews would not be destroyed for another eleven months because he was afraid that the king might change his mind. On the other hand, Hashem wanted the time stretched out for eleven months so that the Jewish people would have time to repent.

14 The letter said that this law should be announced in every country and made known to every nation, so that they should be ready for that day.''

15 The messengers left in a rush, just as the king commanded, and the law was announced in Shushan, the capital city. Achashveirosh and Haman sat down together to drink, but when the Jews of Shushan heard the news they became confused.

יד פַּתְשֶׁגֶן הַכְּתָב לְהִנָּתֵן דָּת בְּכָל־מְדִינָה וּמְדִינָה גָּלוּי לְכָל־הָעַמִּים לִהְיוֹת עֲתִדִים לַיּוֹם הַזֶּה: טו הָרָצִים יָצְאוּ דְחוּפִים בִּדְבַר הַמֶּלֶךְ וְהַדָּת נִתְּנָה בְּשׁוּשַׁן הַבִּירָה וְהַמֶּלֶךְ וְהָמָן יָשְׁבוּ לִשְׁתּוֹת וְהָעִיר שׁוּשָׁן נָבוֹכָה:

A Closer Look

Why were the Jewish people in Shushan confused? We would have expected them to be terrified, but not confused. This is because many of them saw themselves as being true Persians. They were confused because they could not believe their friends, the Persians, wanted to destroy them. Sadly, such has been the confusion of many Jews throughout history.

Chapter Four — פרק ד

א וּמָרְדֳּכַי יָדַע אֶת־כָּל־אֲשֶׁר נַעֲשָׂה
וַיִּקְרַע מָרְדֳּכַי אֶת־בְּגָדָיו וַיִּלְבַּשׁ שַׂק
וָאֵפֶר וַיֵּצֵא בְּתוֹךְ הָעִיר וַיִּזְעַק זְעָקָה
גְדֹלָה וּמָרָה: ב וַיָּבוֹא עַד לִפְנֵי שַׁעַר־
הַמֶּלֶךְ כִּי אֵין לָבוֹא אֶל־שַׁעַר הַמֶּלֶךְ
בִּלְבוּשׁ שָׂק:

[1] Mordechai knew everything that had happened. He tore his clothing and put on sackcloth and ashes. He went out into the city and cried out loudly and bitterly.

[2] He came until outside the king's gate, because no one was allowed to enter the king's gate wearing sackcloth.

Did You Know??

How did Mordechai know about everything that had happened? Our Rabbis teach us that it was he was told in a dream that Heaven had decreed this on the Jews because they bowed to Nebuchadnezzar's idol and enjoyed Achashveirosh's party.

Tearing one's clothing and putting on ashes are signs of mourning.

³ Meanwhile, in every one of the king's countries, in every place where the king's law was sent, the Jews were very sad. They fasted, they cried, and they wailed. Most of the Jews sat on sackcloth and ashes.

⁴ Esther's maids and servants came and told her everything that was happening. The queen became very upset. She sent clothes for Mordechai to put on so that he would take off his sackcloth, but he would not take them.

ג וּבְכָל־מְדִינָה וּמְדִינָה מְקוֹם אֲשֶׁר דְּבַר־הַמֶּלֶךְ וְדָתוֹ מַגִּיעַ אֵבֶל גָּדוֹל לַיְּהוּדִים וְצוֹם וּבְכִי וּמִסְפֵּד שַׂק וָאֵפֶר יֻצַּע לָרַבִּים: ד °וַתְּבוֹאנָה [°ותבואינה כ׳] נַעֲרוֹת אֶסְתֵּר וְסָרִיסֶיהָ וַיַּגִּידוּ לָהּ וַתִּתְחַלְחַל הַמַּלְכָּה מְאֹד וַתִּשְׁלַח בְּגָדִים לְהַלְבִּישׁ אֶת־מָרְדֳּכַי וּלְהָסִיר שַׂקּוֹ מֵעָלָיו וְלֹא קִבֵּל:

A Closer Look
Esther sent Mordechai proper clothing so he would be able to enter the palace and tell her what was going on.

⁵ So Esther called for Hasach, one of the servants that the king had given her. She ordered him to go to Mordechai and find out what was happening.

⁶ Hasach went out to Mordechai, to the main street of the city, in front of the royal gate.

⁷ Mordechai told him all that had happened, and about the money that Haman had promised to give to the royal treasury to have the Jews destroyed.

⁸ Mordechai also gave him a copy of the law that was given out in Shushan, the law that said that all the Jews would be wiped out. He wanted him to show it to Esther and explain to her that she must go before the king to beg and plead for her nation.

ה וַתִּקְרָא אֶסְתֵּר לַהֲתָךְ מִסָּרִיסֵי הַמֶּלֶךְ אֲשֶׁר הֶעֱמִיד לְפָנֶיהָ וַתְּצַוֵּהוּ עַל־מָרְדֳּכָי לָדַעַת מַה־זֶּה וְעַל־מַה־זֶּה: ו וַיֵּצֵא הֲתָךְ אֶל־מָרְדֳּכָי אֶל־רְחוֹב הָעִיר אֲשֶׁר לִפְנֵי שַׁעַר־הַמֶּלֶךְ: ז וַיַּגֶּד־לוֹ מָרְדֳּכַי אֵת כָּל־אֲשֶׁר קָרָהוּ וְאֵת ׀ פָּרָשַׁת הַכֶּסֶף אֲשֶׁר אָמַר הָמָן לִשְׁקוֹל עַל־גִּנְזֵי הַמֶּלֶךְ °בַּיְּהוּדִים [°בַּיְּהוּדִיים כ] לְאַבְּדָם: ח וְאֶת־פַּתְשֶׁגֶן כְּתָב־הַדָּת אֲשֶׁר־נִתַּן בְּשׁוּשָׁן לְהַשְׁמִידָם נָתַן לוֹ לְהַרְאוֹת אֶת־אֶסְתֵּר וּלְהַגִּיד לָהּ וּלְצַוּוֹת עָלֶיהָ לָבוֹא אֶל־הַמֶּלֶךְ לְהִתְחַנֶּן־לוֹ וּלְבַקֵּשׁ מִלְּפָנָיו עַל־עַמָּהּ:

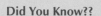

Did You Know??

Some say that Hasach was the prophet Daniel, the same Daniel who had been thrown into the lion's den. He was Esther's faithful servant whom she trusted to keep all her secrets. That is why she was able to send him to talk to Mordechai.

A Closer Look

Mordechai also explained that Esther's role as queen would now take a big change. She would soon have to tell the king exactly who she was and where she was from.

⁹ Hasach came and told Esther what Mordechai had said.

¹⁰ Esther told Hasach to tell Mordechai:

¹¹ "All the king's servants and everyone in the land knows the law that anyone who comes before the king, to his inner court, without being called, will be put to death. Only if the king points his gold scepter at that person may that person live. I have not been called before the king for thirty days."

¹² They told Mordechai what Esther had said.

ט וַיָּבוֹא הֲתָךְ וַיַּגֵּד לְאֶסְתֵּר אֵת דִּבְרֵי מָרְדֳּכָי: י וַתֹּאמֶר אֶסְתֵּר לַהֲתָךְ וַתְּצַוֵּהוּ אֶל־מָרְדֳּכָי: יא כָּל־עַבְדֵי הַמֶּלֶךְ וְעַם מְדִינוֹת הַמֶּלֶךְ יוֹדְעִים אֲשֶׁר כָּל־אִישׁ וְאִשָּׁה אֲשֶׁר־יָבוֹא אֶל־הַמֶּלֶךְ אֶל־הֶחָצֵר הַפְּנִימִית אֲשֶׁר לֹא־יִקָּרֵא אַחַת דָּתוֹ לְהָמִית לְבַד מֵאֲשֶׁר יוֹשִׁיט־לוֹ הַמֶּלֶךְ אֶת־שַׁרְבִיט הַזָּהָב וְחָיָה וַאֲנִי לֹא נִקְרֵאתִי לָבוֹא אֶל־הַמֶּלֶךְ זֶה שְׁלוֹשִׁים יוֹם: יב וַיַּגִּידוּ לְמָרְדֳּכָי אֵת דִּבְרֵי אֶסְתֵּר:

A Closer Look

Esther told Mordechai that even if the king pointed his scepter at her and let her live, it would not be a good time to request something from him. She would already owe the king her life and could not ask for anything else. She explained that it had been thirty days since the king had called for her. He would probably ask to see her soon anyway.

Did You Know??

Hasach did not want to tell Mordechai that Esther did not want to do what he asked. Esther sent someone else to tell Mordechai. We learn from this to try not to bring bad news.

¹³ Mordechai sent back an answer to Esther:

"Do not think you will be saved if the rest of the Jews are killed, just because you are in the king's palace.

¹⁴ "If you remain silent at a time like this, the rescue of the Jews will come from a different place; but you and your father's house will be destroyed. Who knows? It might be just because of a time like this that you were made queen!"

יג וַיֹּאמֶר מָרְדֳּכַי לְהָשִׁיב אֶל־אֶסְתֵּר אַל־תְּדַמִּי בְנַפְשֵׁךְ לְהִמָּלֵט בֵּית־הַמֶּלֶךְ מִכָּל־הַיְּהוּדִים: יד כִּי אִם־הַחֲרֵשׁ תַּחֲרִישִׁי בָּעֵת הַזֹּאת רֶוַח וְהַצָּלָה יַעֲמוֹד לַיְּהוּדִים מִמָּקוֹם אַחֵר וְאַתְּ וּבֵית־אָבִיךְ תֹּאבֵדוּ וּמִי יוֹדֵעַ אִם־לְעֵת כָּזֹאת הִגַּעַתְּ לַמַּלְכוּת:

Did You Know??

The word מָקוֹם means place, and it is also a way of referring to Hashem. In verse 14 Mordechai tells Esther that even if she doesn't help, Hashem will save the Jews.

A Closer Look

Even though the decree to kill the Jews would not take effect for another year, Mordechai did not want Esther to delay seeing the king by even one day. He saw the Jews were ready right now to pray and to do *teshuvah*. Who knew how they would feel tomorrow? And maybe Esther would no longer be queen by then.

Mordechai wanted Esther to understand that even though she was queen, she might not be saved from Haman's evil decree.

15 Esther sent back an answer to Mordechai:

16 "Go and gather together all the Jews of Shushan and fast for me — all of you should not eat or drink for three days and nights. My servants and I will also fast. Then I will go to the king, even though it is against the law. If I die, then I will die."

17 Mordechai left and did just as Esther had told him to do.

טו וַתֹּאמֶר אֶסְתֵּר לְהָשִׁיב אֶל־מָרְדֳּכָי:

טז לֵךְ כְּנוֹס אֶת־כָּל־הַיְּהוּדִים הַנִּמְצְאִים בְּשׁוּשָׁן וְצוּמוּ עָלַי וְאַל־תֹּאכְלוּ וְאַל־תִּשְׁתּוּ שְׁלֹשֶׁת יָמִים לַיְלָה וָיוֹם גַּם־אֲנִי וְנַעֲרֹתַי אָצוּם כֵּן וּבְכֵן אָבוֹא אֶל־הַמֶּלֶךְ אֲשֶׁר לֹא־כַדָּת וְכַאֲשֶׁר אָבַדְתִּי אָבָדְתִּי:

יז וַיַּעֲבֹר מָרְדֳּכָי וַיַּעַשׂ כְּכֹל אֲשֶׁר־צִוְּתָה עָלָיו אֶסְתֵּר:

A Closer Look

Esther wanted the Jewish people to fast to make up for their sin of eating and drinking at Achashveirosh's royal party.

Esther told Mordechai to gather the Jews together. When a group prays together, its prayers are stronger.

The Jewish people did teshuvah and Hashem forgave them. The story of Purim now takes a whole new turn.

Did You Know??

Haman's letter was written on the 13th day of Nissan, two days before Pesach. The three-day fast went into Pesach.

Many thousands of Jews — men, women, and children — gathered together in the streets of Shushan. They brought Mordechai a Torah which was wrapped in sackcloth, and he read the section telling the Jewish people how, when things are difficult, they can return to Hashem and He will have mercy on them. He told them the story of Yonah and the city of Nineveh. Hashem was going to destroy the whole city, but when they did *teshuvah,* Hashem accepted it and took back His decree.

Chapter Five — פרק ה

¹ **O**n the third day, Esther dressed in her royal clothing and stood in the inner courtyard of the king's palace, opposite the king's room. The king was sitting on the royal throne, facing the entrance to the room.

² As soon as the king saw Queen Esther standing in the courtyard, he was happy with her. The king pointed the golden scepter that was in his hand at Esther. She approached the king and touched the tip of his scepter.

א וַיְהִ֣י ׀ בַּיּ֣וֹם הַשְּׁלִישִׁ֗י וַתִּלְבַּ֤שׁ אֶסְתֵּר֙ מַלְכ֔וּת וַֽתַּעֲמֹ֔ד בַּחֲצַ֣ר בֵּית־הַמֶּ֫לֶךְ הַפְּנִימִ֗ית נֹ֚כַח בֵּ֣ית הַמֶּ֔לֶךְ וְהַמֶּ֗לֶךְ יוֹשֵׁ֞ב עַל־כִּסֵּ֤א מַלְכוּתוֹ֙ בְּבֵ֣ית הַמַּלְכ֔וּת נֹ֖כַח פֶּ֥תַח הַבָּֽיִת: ב וַיְהִי֩ כִרְא֨וֹת הַמֶּ֜לֶךְ אֶת־אֶסְתֵּ֣ר הַמַּלְכָּ֗ה עֹמֶ֨דֶת֙ בֶּֽחָצֵ֔ר נָשְׂאָ֥ה חֵ֖ן בְּעֵינָ֑יו וַיּ֨וֹשֶׁט הַמֶּ֜לֶךְ לְאֶסְתֵּ֗ר אֶת־שַׁרְבִ֤יט הַזָּהָב֙ אֲשֶׁ֣ר בְּיָד֔וֹ וַתִּקְרַ֣ב אֶסְתֵּ֔ר וַתִּגַּ֖ע בְּרֹ֥אשׁ הַשַּׁרְבִֽיט:

Did You Know??

At first, Achashveirosh became very angry when he saw Esther coming, despite his orders that no one come in without being called. But Hashem made a miracle and Esther found favor in the eyes of Achashveirosh. He told her that the law about no one coming to him did not apply to her, since she was his special wife.

³ The king said to her:

"What is it, Esther my queen? What do you want? You can have anything you want, up to half of my kingdom."

⁴ Esther said:

"If it finds favor with the king, I would like the king and Haman to come today to the party that I have made for him."

⁵ The king said, "Rush Haman to do what Esther said." Then the king and Haman came to the party that Esther had made.

ג וַיֹּאמֶר לָהּ הַמֶּלֶךְ מַה־לָּךְ אֶסְתֵּר הַמַּלְכָּה וּמַה־בַּקָּשָׁתֵךְ עַד־חֲצִי הַמַּלְכוּת וְיִנָּתֵן לָךְ: ד וַתֹּאמֶר אֶסְתֵּר אִם־עַל־הַמֶּלֶךְ טוֹב יָבוֹא הַמֶּלֶךְ וְהָמָן הַיּוֹם אֶל־הַמִּשְׁתֶּה אֲשֶׁר־עָשִׂיתִי לוֹ: ה וַיֹּאמֶר הַמֶּלֶךְ מַהֲרוּ אֶת־הָמָן לַעֲשׂוֹת אֶת־דְּבַר אֶסְתֵּר וַיָּבֹא הַמֶּלֶךְ וְהָמָן אֶל־הַמִּשְׁתֶּה אֲשֶׁר־עָשְׂתָה אֶסְתֵּר:

Did You Know??

The king offered Esther "half the kingdom," but not the "whole kingdom." Our Sages teach us that this means that he would have given her anything except the right to rebuild the *Beis HaMikdash* in Jerusalem, which was at the center of his empire.

A Closer Look

Esther had many reasons for inviting Haman. One was that she wanted Achashveirosh and the other ministers to be jealous and suspicious of Haman. Another reason was that she wanted the Jews to continue to pray and do *teshuvah,* not to rely on the Jewish queen to help them.

⁶ During the party, the king said to Esther: "What would you like to ask for? I will give it to you. What do you desire? Even up to half of the kingdom, it will be done."

⁷ Esther answered and said:
"This is what I would like to ask for, and this is what I desire.

⁸ "If I have found favor in the eyes of the king and the king would like to fulfill any request, let the king and Haman come to the party that I will make for them. Tomorrow, I will do what the king has asked."

וַיֹּ֨אמֶר הַמֶּ֤לֶךְ לְאֶסְתֵּר֙ בְּמִשְׁתֵּ֣ה הַיַּ֔יִן מַה־שְּׁאֵלָתֵ֖ךְ וְיִנָּ֣תֵֽן לָ֑ךְ וּמַה־בַּקָּשָׁתֵ֛ךְ עַד־חֲצִ֥י הַמַּלְכ֖וּת וְתֵעָֽשׂ׃ וַתַּ֤עַן אֶסְתֵּר֙ וַתֹּאמַ֔ר שְׁאֵלָתִ֖י וּבַקָּשָׁתִֽי׃ אִם־מָצָ֨אתִי חֵ֜ן בְּעֵינֵ֣י הַמֶּ֗לֶךְ וְאִם־עַל־הַמֶּ֨לֶךְ֙ ט֔וֹב לָתֵת֙ אֶת־שְׁאֵ֣לָתִ֔י וְלַעֲשׂ֖וֹת אֶת־בַּקָּשָׁתִ֑י יָב֧וֹא הַמֶּ֛לֶךְ וְהָמָ֖ן אֶל־הַמִּשְׁתֶּ֣ה אֲשֶׁ֣ר אֶֽעֱשֶׂ֣ה לָהֶ֔ם וּמָחָ֥ר אֶֽעֱשֶׂ֖ה כִּדְבַ֥ר הַמֶּֽלֶךְ׃

Did You Know??
When Esther said she would do what the king asked, she meant that she would finally tell him where she was from.

⁹ Haman went out that day happy and in a good mood. But when Haman saw Mordechai at the king's gate, and Mordechai did not stand up, or even move for him, Haman became very angry at him.

ט וַיֵּצֵא הָמָן בַּיּוֹם הַהוּא שָׂמֵחַ וְטוֹב לֵב וְכִרְאוֹת הָמָן אֶת־מָרְדְּכַי בְּשַׁעַר הַמֶּלֶךְ וְלֹא־קָם וְלֹא־זָע מִמֶּנּוּ וַיִּמָּלֵא הָמָן עַל־מָרְדְּכַי חֵמָה:

A Closer Look

Haman left the party feeling more important than ever. He was the most powerful minister. He had money. He had a large family. And now even the queen honored him by inviting him to her private party with the king.

Now his downfall was about to start.

¹⁰ Haman held in his anger and went home. He brought his friends and his wife, Zeresh.

¹¹ Haman told them how proud he was of his great wealth and his many children. And he told them how the king had given him a powerful position in the government — more important than any other official or servant of the king.

י וַיִּתְאַפַּק הָמָן וַיָּבוֹא אֶל־בֵּיתוֹ וַיִּשְׁלַח וַיָּבֵא אֶת־אֹהֲבָיו וְאֶת־זֶרֶשׁ אִשְׁתּוֹ:

יא וַיְסַפֵּר לָהֶם הָמָן אֶת־כְּבוֹד עָשְׁרוֹ וְרֹב בָּנָיו וְאֵת כָּל־אֲשֶׁר גִּדְּלוֹ הַמֶּלֶךְ וְאֵת אֲשֶׁר נִשְּׂאוֹ עַל־הַשָּׂרִים וְעַבְדֵי הַמֶּלֶךְ:

¹² Haman said:

"Besides all this, I was the only one whom Queen Esther brought to the private party that she made with the king. And tomorrow, too, only I and the king are invited by her.

¹³ "But this is all worthless to me as long as I see Mordechai the Jew sitting at the king's gate."

יב וַיֹּאמֶר הָמָן אַף לֹא־הֵבִיאָה אֶסְתֵּר הַמַּלְכָּה עִם־הַמֶּלֶךְ אֶל־הַמִּשְׁתֶּה אֲשֶׁר־עָשָׂתָה כִּי אִם־אוֹתִי וְגַם־לְמָחָר אֲנִי קָרוּא־לָהּ עִם־הַמֶּלֶךְ: יג וְכָל־זֶה אֵינֶנּוּ שֹׁוֶה לִי בְּכָל־עֵת אֲשֶׁר אֲנִי רֹאֶה אֶת־מָרְדֳּכַי הַיְּהוּדִי יוֹשֵׁב בְּשַׁעַר הַמֶּלֶךְ:

Did You Know??

Fifty cubits is about as tall as an eight-floor-high building. It is about a hundred feet high. Haman wanted the gallows to be very high so that he would be able to see it from Queen Esther's party.

That same night, Haman himself called carpenters to come and build the gallows right away. He and his sons helped them.

A Closer Look

That evening, Haman saw Mordechai learning with thousands of young children. Haman had these children tied in chains, and placed guards to watch them. He said that in the morning he would kill them before he hanged Mordechai. The children cried to Hashem and their tears ripped through the Gates of Heaven. The evil decree against the Jewish people was then torn up.

יד וַתֹּאמֶר לוֹ זֶרֶשׁ אִשְׁתּוֹ וְכָל־אֹהֲבָיו
יַעֲשׂוּ־עֵץ גָּבֹהַּ חֲמִשִּׁים אַמָּה וּבַבֹּקֶר ׀
אֱמֹר לַמֶּלֶךְ וְיִתְלוּ אֶת־מָרְדֳּכַי עָלָיו וּבֹא
עִם־הַמֶּלֶךְ אֶל־הַמִּשְׁתֶּה שָׂמֵחַ וַיִּיטַב
הַדָּבָר לִפְנֵי הָמָן וַיַּעַשׂ הָעֵץ:

14 Haman's wife, Zeresh, and all his friends said to him:

"Make a gallows fifty cubits high. In the morning tell the king that they should hang Mordechai on it. Then you can go with the king to the party and be happy."

Haman liked the idea, and he built the gallows.

Did You Know??

Zeresh, Haman's wife, told him that the only way to win against Mordechai and the Jewish people was by creating a brand new punishment — a punishment that had never yet been given to the Jews. She pointed out that righteous Jews had been saved from many types of punishments, among them a fiery furnace (Avraham), the sword (Yitzchak at the *Akeidah*), drowning (the Jews at the Reed Sea), a lion's den (Daniel), and a dungeon (Yosef). But no Jew had yet been saved from hanging.

Chapter Six — פרק ו

On that night, the king could not sleep. He asked that the book of records — the book of his own history — be brought and read to him.

2 In it was found written that Mordechai had saved the king from Bigsan and Teresh, two of the king's servants, guards of the entrance to the palace, who had tried to kill King Achashveirosh.

א בַּלַּיְלָה הַהוּא נָדְדָה שְׁנַת הַמֶּלֶךְ וַיֹּאמֶר לְהָבִיא אֶת־סֵפֶר הַזִּכְרֹנוֹת דִּבְרֵי הַיָּמִים וַיִּהְיוּ נִקְרָאִים לִפְנֵי הַמֶּלֶךְ: ב וַיִּמָּצֵא כָתוּב אֲשֶׁר הִגִּיד מָרְדֳּכַי עַל־בִּגְתָנָא וָתֶרֶשׁ שְׁנֵי סָרִיסֵי הַמֶּלֶךְ מִשֹּׁמְרֵי הַסַּף אֲשֶׁר בִּקְשׁוּ לִשְׁלֹחַ יָד בַּמֶּלֶךְ אֲחַשְׁוֵרוֹשׁ:

A Closer Look

Our Sages teach us that Achashveirosh was not the only king who could not sleep. Hashem, the King of kings, also could not rest, so to speak, because His people, the Jewish people, was in danger.

Did You Know??

King Achashveirosh could not sleep because he kept seeing a picture of Haman holding a sword and trying to kill him. He thought about the fact that Esther had invited Haman to the private party. Maybe the two of them were plotting to kill him?!

Everyone was busy that night; Haman inspecting the gallows,
Esther preparing for the party, and Mordechai learning and praying.

Did You Know??
The person reading the Megillah raises his voice at this point because the main miracle of Purim begins now.

³ The king asked:

"What honor has been given to Mordechai because of this?"

"Nothing has been done for him," his servants replied.

⁴ Then the king said, "Who is in the courtyard?" Haman had just arrived to the king's outer courtyard to tell the king to hang Mordechai on the gallows that he had prepared for him!

⁵ The king's servants answered him, "It is Haman standing in the courtyard." "Let him come in," said the king.

⁶ Haman came in, and the king said to him, "What should be done to the man whom the king wishes to honor?" Haman thought to himself, "Who could the king possibly wish to honor more than me?"

ג וַיֹּאמֶר הַמֶּלֶךְ מַה־נַּעֲשָׂה יְקָר וּגְדוּלָּה לְמָרְדֳּכַי עַל־זֶה וַיֹּאמְרוּ נַעֲרֵי הַמֶּלֶךְ מְשָׁרְתָיו לֹא־נַעֲשָׂה עִמּוֹ דָּבָר: ד וַיֹּאמֶר הַמֶּלֶךְ מִי בֶחָצֵר וְהָמָן בָּא לַחֲצַר בֵּית־הַמֶּלֶךְ הַחִיצוֹנָה לֵאמֹר לַמֶּלֶךְ לִתְלוֹת אֶת־מָרְדֳּכַי עַל־הָעֵץ אֲשֶׁר־הֵכִין לוֹ: ה וַיֹּאמְרוּ נַעֲרֵי הַמֶּלֶךְ אֵלָיו הִנֵּה הָמָן עֹמֵד בֶּחָצֵר וַיֹּאמֶר הַמֶּלֶךְ יָבוֹא: ו וַיָּבוֹא הָמָן וַיֹּאמֶר לוֹ הַמֶּלֶךְ מַה־לַעֲשׂוֹת בָּאִישׁ אֲשֶׁר הַמֶּלֶךְ חָפֵץ בִּיקָרוֹ וַיֹּאמֶר הָמָן בְּלִבּוֹ לְמִי יַחְפֹּץ הַמֶּלֶךְ לַעֲשׂוֹת יְקָר יוֹתֵר מִמֶּנִּי:

A Closer Look

At this point in the story, Achashveirosh began to suspect that Haman was trying to kill him. Earlier, he kept dreaming that Haman was trying to kill him. Now Haman was coming in middle of the night.

The king had a selfish reason for wanting to honor Mordechai. If people found out that Mordechai had saved the king's life and was not rewarded, then they would have no reason or desire to help the king.

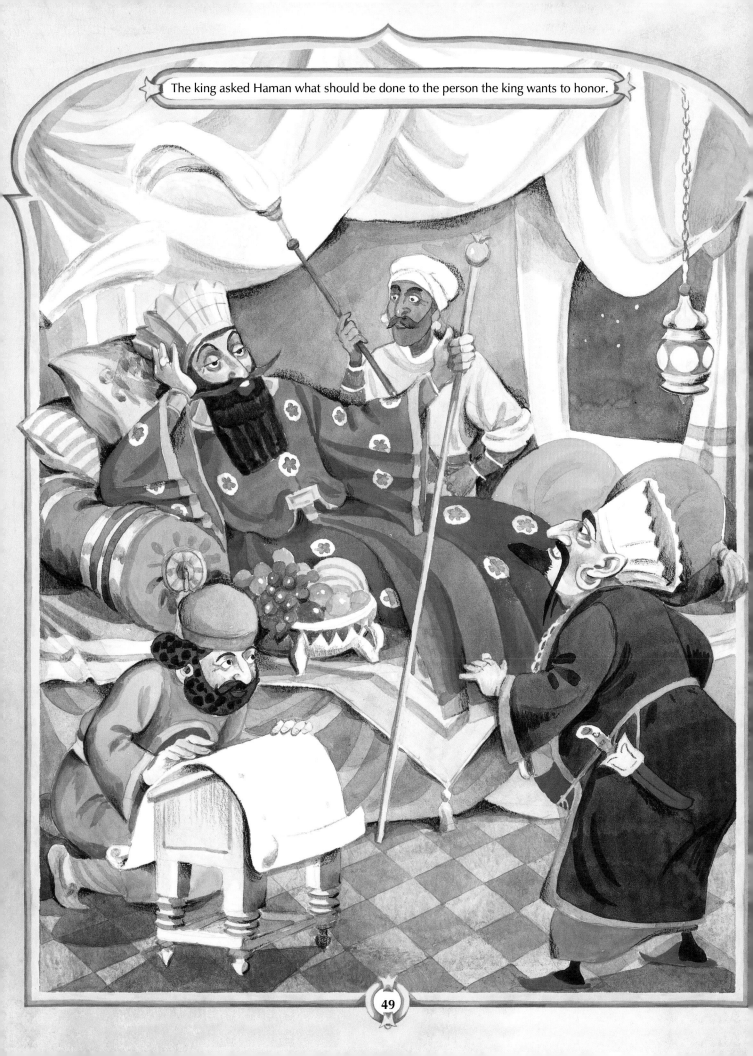

The king asked Haman what should be done to the person the king wants to honor.

⁷ So Haman said to the king:

"(I will tell you what should be done) to the man whom the king wishes to honor.

⁸ "They should bring a royal garment that the king himself has worn, a horse that the king has ridden upon, with the royal crown placed on his head.

⁹ "One of the king's most important officers should take this clothing and the horse and dress this man whom the king wishes to honor. Then the officer should lead the man on the horse throughout the main street of the city while calling out: 'This shall be done to the man whom the king wishes to honor!'"

זוַיֹּ֤אמֶר הָמָן֙ אֶל־הַמֶּ֔לֶךְ אִ֕ישׁ אֲשֶׁ֥ר הַמֶּ֖לֶךְ חָפֵ֥ץ בִּיקָרֽוֹ: חיָבִ֙יאוּ֙ לְב֣וּשׁ מַלְכ֔וּת אֲשֶׁ֥ר לָֽבַשׁ־בּ֖וֹ הַמֶּ֑לֶךְ וְס֗וּס אֲשֶׁ֙ר רָכַ֤ב עָלָיו֙ הַמֶּ֔לֶךְ וַאֲשֶׁ֥ר נִתַּ֛ן כֶּ֥תֶר מַלְכ֖וּת בְּרֹאשֽׁוֹ: טוְנָת֨וֹן הַלְּב֜וּשׁ וְהַסּ֗וּס עַל־יַד־אִ֞ישׁ מִשָּׂרֵ֤י הַמֶּ֙לֶךְ֙ הַֽפַּרְתְּמִ֔ים וְהִלְבִּ֙ישׁוּ֙ אֶת־הָאִ֔ישׁ אֲשֶׁ֥ר הַמֶּ֖לֶךְ חָפֵ֣ץ בִּֽיקָר֑וֹ וְהִרְכִּיבֻ֤הוּ עַל־הַסּוּס֙ בִּרְח֣וֹב הָעִ֔יר וְקָרְא֣וּ לְפָנָ֔יו כָּ֚כָה יֵעָשֶׂ֣ה לָאִ֔ישׁ אֲשֶׁ֥ר הַמֶּ֖לֶךְ חָפֵ֥ץ בִּיקָרֽוֹ:

Did You Know??

At first, Haman mentioned wearing the king's crown. But he saw that as soon as he said "crown" the king got very upset. That is why when he continued speaking, he mentioned only the royal clothes and horses, not the crown.

¹⁰ The king then said to Haman:

"Hurry up! Get the royal garment and the horse that you just spoke about, and do everything that you said to Mordechai, the Jew, who is sitting at the king's gate! Do not leave out even one thing that you mentioned."

יוַיֹּאמֶר הַמֶּלֶךְ לְהָמָן מַהֵר קַח אֶת־הַלְּבוּשׁ וְאֶת־הַסּוּס כַּאֲשֶׁר דִּבַּרְתָּ וַעֲשֵׂה־כֵן לְמָרְדֳּכַי הַיְּהוּדִי הַיּוֹשֵׁב בְּשַׁעַר הַמֶּלֶךְ אַל־תַּפֵּל דָּבָר מִכֹּל אֲשֶׁר דִּבַּרְתָּ:

A Closer Look

When the king said, "Do everything that you said to Mordechai," Haman answered, "Which Mordechai?" "Mordechai the Jew," answered the king. "But there are many Mordechais!" said Haman. "The one who is sitting at the king's gate." Achashveirosh was leaving no room for misunderstanding.

Did You Know??

Achashveirosh wanted Haman to hurry so that he would be ready in time for Queen Esther's party.

51

¹¹ Haman took the garment and the horse and he dressed Mordechai. Then he led him through the main street of the city, and called out before him, "So shall be done to the man whom the king wishes to honor!"

יא וַיִּקַּח הָמָן אֶת־הַלְּבוּשׁ וְאֶת־הַסּוּס וַיַּלְבֵּשׁ אֶת־מָרְדֳּכָי וַיַּרְכִּיבֵהוּ בִּרְחוֹב הָעִיר וַיִּקְרָא לְפָנָיו כָּכָה יֵעָשֶׂה לָאִישׁ אֲשֶׁר הַמֶּלֶךְ חָפֵץ בִּיקָרוֹ:

Did You Know??

The clothes Mordechai was given to wear were the clothes Achashveirosh wore when he was crowned king of Persia. The horse was the horse Achashveirosh rode when he was crowned king.

A Closer Look

Step by step Haman is being brought closer to his downfall. Even though the Name of Hashem is never mentioned outright in the Megillah, we clearly see how He is making everything happen.

Did You Know??

Haman's daughter was standing on the roof when she saw that one person was leading another one on a horse and calling out, "So shall be done to a man whom the king wishes to honor!" She thought that it must be Mordechai leading her father on the horse. She threw a pot filled with garbage onto the man leading the horse. When she realized that she had thrown it on her father, she fell off the roof and died.

12 Mordechai returned to the king's gate while Haman rushed home, sad, and with his head hanging down in shame.

13 Haman told his wife, Zeresh, and all his friends everything that had happened to him. His advisers and his wife, Zeresh, told him:

"If Mordechai is Jewish and you are starting to lose to him, you will not be able to succeed against him. You will definitely lose to him."

14 While they were still talking to him, the king's guards came. They rushed Haman to the party that Queen Esther had made.

יב וַיָּשָׁב מָרְדֳּכַי אֶל־שַׁעַר הַמֶּלֶךְ וְהָמָן נִדְחַף אֶל־בֵּיתוֹ אָבֵל וַחֲפוּי רֹאשׁ: יג וַיְסַפֵּר הָמָן לְזֶרֶשׁ אִשְׁתּוֹ וּלְכָל־אֹהֲבָיו אֵת כָּל־אֲשֶׁר קָרָהוּ וַיֹּאמְרוּ לוֹ חֲכָמָיו וְזֶרֶשׁ אִשְׁתּוֹ אִם מִזֶּרַע הַיְּהוּדִים מָרְדֳּכַי אֲשֶׁר הַחִלּוֹתָ לִנְפֹּל לְפָנָיו לֹא־תוּכַל לוֹ כִּי־נָפוֹל תִּפּוֹל לְפָנָיו: יד עוֹדָם מְדַבְּרִים עִמּוֹ וְסָרִיסֵי הַמֶּלֶךְ הִגִּיעוּ וַיַּבְהִלוּ לְהָבִיא אֶת־הָמָן אֶל־הַמִּשְׁתֶּה אֲשֶׁר־עָשְׂתָה אֶסְתֵּר:

Did You Know??

Haman's advisers told him to quickly take apart the gallows, before it could be used against him. Hashem stopped this by having the guards come and rush him away to the queen's party.

A Closer Look

Haman's wife and friends were still in his house because they wanted to know if he succeeded in having Mordechai killed.

First, these people were called his friends, but then they were called his advisers. This is because they were friendly to Haman only because of his power. Once they saw his downfall coming, they deserted him and told him he would fail.

Chapter Seven — פרק ז

¹ The king and Haman came to the party with Queen Esther.

² The king said to Esther again, on the second day, at the wine party:

"What is your desire, Esther the queen, and it will be given to you. Whatever you ask, up to half of my kingdom, will be done."

³ Queen Esther answered:

"If I find favor in your eyes, O King, and if it pleases the King, to save my life is my request. That my nation be saved is my desire.

⁴ "For I and my people have been sold, to be killed and destroyed. Now, if we would have just been sold as slaves, I would have kept quiet. But the enemy is causing terrible damage to the king."

אוַיָּבֹא הַמֶּלֶךְ וְהָמָן לִשְׁתּוֹת עִם־אֶסְתֵּר הַמַּלְכָּה: בוַיֹּאמֶר הַמֶּלֶךְ לְאֶסְתֵּר גַּם בַּיּוֹם הַשֵּׁנִי בְּמִשְׁתֵּה הַיַּיִן מַה־שְּׁאֵלָתֵךְ אֶסְתֵּר הַמַּלְכָּה וְתִנָּתֵן לָךְ וּמַה־בַּקָּשָׁתֵךְ עַד־חֲצִי הַמַּלְכוּת וְתֵעָשׂ: גוַתַּעַן אֶסְתֵּר הַמַּלְכָּה וַתֹּאמַר אִם־מָצָאתִי חֵן בְּעֵינֶיךָ הַמֶּלֶךְ וְאִם־עַל־הַמֶּלֶךְ טוֹב תִּנָּתֶן־לִי נַפְשִׁי בִּשְׁאֵלָתִי וְעַמִּי בְּבַקָּשָׁתִי: דכִּי נִמְכַּרְנוּ אֲנִי וְעַמִּי לְהַשְׁמִיד לַהֲרוֹג וּלְאַבֵּד וְאִלּוּ לַעֲבָדִים וְלִשְׁפָחוֹת נִמְכַּרְנוּ הֶחֱרַשְׁתִּי כִּי אֵין הַצָּר שֹׁוֶה בְּנֵזֶק הַמֶּלֶךְ:

A Closer Look

When Esther made her request to Achashveirosh, she used the word "King" twice. She was not only speaking to Achashveirosh, she was also praying to Hashem, King of the Universe, begging him to save His Jewish people.

5 King Achashveirosh then spoke, and he said to Queen Esther, "Who is this person? Where is the person who has tried to do this terrible thing?

6 And Esther said, "It is an adversary and an enemy; it is this evil Haman." Haman shook in fear before the king and queen.

הוַיֹּ֙אמֶר֙ הַמֶּ֣לֶךְ אֲחַשְׁוֵר֔וֹשׁ וַיֹּ֖אמֶר לְאֶסְתֵּ֣ר הַמַּלְכָּ֑ה מִ֣י ה֤וּא זֶה֙ וְאֵֽי־זֶ֣ה ה֔וּא אֲשֶׁר־מְלָא֥וֹ לִבּ֖וֹ לַעֲשׂ֥וֹת כֵּֽן: וַתֹּ֣אמֶר אֶסְתֵּ֔ר אִ֚ישׁ צַ֣ר וְאוֹיֵ֔ב הָמָ֥ן הָרָ֖ע הַזֶּ֑ה וְהָמָ֣ן נִבְעַ֔ת מִלִּפְנֵ֥י הַמֶּ֖לֶךְ וְהַמַּלְכָּֽה:

Did You Know??

Achashveirosh left the room to calm down. But in the garden he saw angels who looked like workers, and they were pulling out trees from his garden. When Achashveirosh asked them what they were doing, they answered that Haman had given them this job.

A Closer Look

Didn't Achashveirosh know of Haman's plan? After all, he gave Haman permission to carry it out! Some explain that since Achashverosh did not know that Esther was Jewish, he did not realize that Haman's plan would include her. Some say that Achashveirosh did not tell Haman that he could wipe out the Jews, he only told him to do whatever he wanted with them. That is why this came as a surprise to Achashveirosh.

7 The king stood up in anger. He left the wine party and walked out to the palace garden. Haman stayed behind to beg Queen Esther to save his life, because he saw that the king had already decided to kill him.

8 When the king returned from the palace garden to the wine party, Haman was falling on the queen's couch. The king said, "Are you attacking the queen even when I am in the house?!" As soon as the king said this, they covered Haman's face.

9 Then Charvonah, one of the king's servants, said:

"There are also gallows that Haman made to hang Mordechai, who had spoken to help the king. They are at Haman's house and they are fifty cubits high."

"Hang him on it!" ordered the king.

10 They hanged Haman on the gallows that he had prepared for Mordechai. And the king's anger quieted down.

ז וְהַמֶּ֣לֶךְ קָ֣ם בַּחֲמָתוֹ֩ מִמִּשְׁתֵּ֨ה הַיַּ֜יִן אֶל־גִּנַּ֣ת הַבִּיתָ֗ן וְהָמָ֣ן עָמַ֗ד לְבַקֵּ֤שׁ עַל־נַפְשׁוֹ֙ מֵֽאֶסְתֵּ֣ר הַמַּלְכָּ֔ה כִּ֣י רָאָ֔ה כִּֽי־כָלְתָ֧ה אֵלָ֛יו הָרָעָ֖ה מֵאֵ֥ת הַמֶּֽלֶךְ: ח וְהַמֶּ֣לֶךְ שָׁ֞ב מִגִּנַּ֣ת הַבִּיתָן֮ אֶל־בֵּ֣ית ׀ מִשְׁתֵּ֣ה הַיַּיִן֒ וְהָמָן֙ נֹפֵ֔ל עַל־הַמִּטָּה֙ אֲשֶׁ֣ר אֶסְתֵּ֣ר עָלֶ֔יהָ וַיֹּ֣אמֶר הַמֶּ֔לֶךְ הֲ֠גַם לִכְבּ֧וֹשׁ אֶת־הַמַּלְכָּ֛ה עִמִּ֖י בַּבָּ֑יִת הַדָּבָ֗ר יָצָא֙ מִפִּ֣י הַמֶּ֔לֶךְ וּפְנֵ֥י הָמָ֖ן חָפֽוּ: ט וַיֹּ֣אמֶר חַרְבוֹנָ֣ה אֶחָ֣ד מִן־הַסָּרִיסִ֞ים לִפְנֵ֣י הַמֶּ֗לֶךְ גַּ֣ם הִנֵּֽה־הָעֵ֣ץ אֲשֶׁר־עָשָׂ֪ה הָמָ֟ן לְֽמָרְדֳּכַ֞י אֲשֶׁ֧ר דִּבֶּר־ט֣וֹב עַל־הַמֶּ֗לֶךְ עֹמֵד֙ בְּבֵ֣ית הָמָ֔ן גָּבֹ֖הַּ חֲמִשִּׁ֣ים אַמָּ֑ה וַיֹּ֥אמֶר הַמֶּ֖לֶךְ תְּלֻ֥הוּ עָלָֽיו: י וַיִּתְלוּ֙ אֶת־הָמָ֔ן עַל־הָעֵ֖ץ אֲשֶׁר־הֵכִ֣ין לְמָרְדֳּכָ֑י וַחֲמַ֥ת הַמֶּ֖לֶךְ שָׁכָֽכָה:

A Closer Look
Because of Charvonah's quick action, Haman did not have time to come up with a way to save himself.

Did You Know??
At first, Charvonah was involved in Haman's plan to kill Mordechai. When he saw that Haman was doomed, he quickly switched sides and became Haman's enemy. He is the one who recommended that Haman be hanged from his own gallows.

Did You Know??
Actually, Haman was standing in front of Queen Esther's couch to beg her for mercy. As Achashveirosh walked back into the room, an angel came and pushed Haman, so that it would seem like he was attacking the queen.

Chapter Eight — פרק ח

¹ **O**n that day, King Achashveirosh gave the property of Haman, the enemy of the Jews, to Queen Esther. Mordechai then came before the king, because Esther now told Achashveirosh that she and Mordechai were related.

² The king took the royal ring that he had taken from Haman, and gave it to Mordechai. Esther put Mordechai in charge of Haman's property.

א בַּיּוֹם הַהוּא נָתַן הַמֶּלֶךְ אֲחַשְׁוֵרוֹשׁ לְאֶסְתֵּר הַמַּלְכָּה אֶת־בֵּית הָמָן צֹרֵר הַיְּהוּדִים [°הַיְּהוּדִיים כ] וּמָרְדְּכַי בָּא לִפְנֵי הַמֶּלֶךְ כִּי־הִגִּידָה אֶסְתֵּר מָה הוּא־לָהּ: ב וַיָּסַר הַמֶּלֶךְ אֶת־טַבַּעְתּוֹ אֲשֶׁר הֶעֱבִיר מֵהָמָן וַיִּתְּנָהּ לְמָרְדֳּכָי וַתָּשֶׂם אֶסְתֵּר אֶת־מָרְדֳּכַי עַל־בֵּית הָמָן:

A Closer Look
Haman was killed but all was not well. The decree to destroy all the Jews in another 11 months was still in effect. Something had to be done to overturn this decree.

³ Esther spoke to the king again. She fell at his feet and cried, begging him to overturn Haman the Agagite's evil decree, and his plan against the Jews.

⁴ The king pointed his golden scepter at Esther. Esther got up and stood in front of the king.

⁵ She said:

"If it is acceptable to the king, and if he is pleased with me, and if he thinks it proper, and I am good in his eyes, let a law be written to bring back the letters that Haman sent out about his plan; where he wrote to destroy the Jewish people in all the lands of the king.

⁶ "Because how can I bear to see all the evil that will happen to my people?! And how can I bear to watch my family be destroyed?"

גַּוַתּ֣וֹסֶף אֶסְתֵּ֗ר וַתְּדַבֵּר֙ לִפְנֵ֣י הַמֶּ֔לֶךְ וַתִּפֹּ֖ל לִפְנֵ֣י רַגְלָ֑יו וַתֵּ֣בְךְּ וַתִּתְחַנֶּן־ל֗וֹ לְהַעֲבִיר֙ אֶת־רָעַת֙ הָמָ֣ן הָֽאֲגָגִ֔י וְאֵת֙ מַֽחֲשַׁבְתּ֔וֹ אֲשֶׁ֥ר חָשַׁ֖ב עַל־הַיְּהוּדִֽים: דוַיּ֧וֹשֶׁט הַמֶּ֛לֶךְ לְאֶסְתֵּ֖ר אֵ֣ת שַׁרְבִ֣ט הַזָּהָ֑ב וַתָּ֣קָם אֶסְתֵּ֔ר וַֽתַּעֲמֹ֖ד לִפְנֵ֥י הַמֶּֽלֶךְ: הוַ֠תֹּאמֶר אִם־עַל־הַמֶּ֨לֶךְ ט֜וֹב וְאִם־מָצָ֧אתִי חֵ֣ן לְפָנָ֗יו וְכָשֵׁ֤ר הַדָּבָר֙ לִפְנֵ֣י הַמֶּ֔לֶךְ וְטוֹבָ֥ה אֲנִ֖י בְּעֵינָ֑יו יִכָּתֵ֞ב לְהָשִׁ֣יב אֶת־הַסְּפָרִ֗ים מַֽחֲשֶׁ֜בֶת הָמָ֣ן בֶּֽן־הַמְּדָ֗תָא הָֽאֲגָגִי֙ אֲשֶׁ֣ר כָּתַ֔ב לְאַבֵּד֙ אֶת־הַיְּהוּדִ֔ים אֲשֶׁ֖ר בְּכָל־מְדִינ֥וֹת הַמֶּֽלֶךְ: וכִּ֠י אֵֽיכָכָ֤ה אוּכַל֙ וְֽרָאִ֔יתִי בָּֽרָעָ֖ה אֲשֶׁר־יִמְצָ֣א אֶת־עַמִּ֑י וְאֵֽיכָכָ֤ה אוּכַל֙ וְֽרָאִ֔יתִי בְּאָבְדַ֖ן מֽוֹלַדְתִּֽי:

A Closer Look
Esther explained to Achashveirosh that even if he allowed her to live, she could not bear to have her nation killed.

7 King Achashveirosh then said to Queen Esther and to Mordechai the Jew:

"Look, I have given Haman's property to Esther. And he was hanged on the gallows because he plotted against the Jews.

8 "You may write in the name of the king any law you want about the Jewish people, and you may seal it with the king's ring. But any letter that was written and sealed in the king's name cannot be taken back."

9 The king's scribes were called then, on the twenty-third day of the third month, which is the month of Sivan. They wrote just what Mordechai told them to the Jews, to the rulers, the governors, and the officers of the countries from Hodu to Cush, one hundred twenty-seven countries. Each country's letter was in its own alphabet and in its own language; and the Jews' was in their own alphabet and language.

10 And he wrote this in the name of King Achashveirosh and sealed it with the king's ring. He sent out these letters with messengers on very fast horses and very fast camels.

ז וַיֹּ֨אמֶר הַמֶּ֤לֶךְ אֲחַשְׁוֵרֹשׁ֙ לְאֶסְתֵּ֣ר הַמַּלְכָּ֔ה וּֽלְמָרְדֳּכַ֖י הַיְּהוּדִ֑י הִנֵּ֨ה בֵית־הָמָ֜ן נָתַ֣תִּי לְאֶסְתֵּ֗ר וְאֹתוֹ֙ תָּל֣וּ עַל־הָעֵ֔ץ עַ֛ל אֲשֶׁר־שָׁלַ֥ח יָד֖וֹ בַּיְּהוּדִֽים [ביהודיים]: ח וְאַתֶּ֡ם כִּתְב֣וּ עַל־הַיְּהוּדִ֡ים כַּטּוֹב֩ בְּעֵֽינֵיכֶ֨ם בְּשֵׁ֤ם הַמֶּ֨לֶךְ֙ וְחִתְמ֣וּ בְּטַבַּ֣עַת הַמֶּ֔לֶךְ כִּֽי־כְתָ֞ב אֲשֶׁר־נִכְתָּ֣ב בְּשֵׁם־הַמֶּ֗לֶךְ וְנַחְתּ֛וֹם בְּטַבַּ֥עַת הַמֶּ֖לֶךְ אֵ֥ין לְהָשִֽׁיב: ט וַיִּקָּרְא֣וּ סֹפְרֵי־הַמֶּ֣לֶךְ בָּֽעֵת־הַהִ֗יא בַּחֹ֣דֶשׁ הַשְּׁלִישִׁ֡י הוּא־חֹ֣דֶשׁ סִיוָ֡ן בִּשְׁלוֹשָׁ֣ה וְעֶשְׂרִים֮ בּוֹ֒ וַיִּכָּתֵ֣ב כְּֽכָל־אֲשֶׁר־צִוָּ֣ה מָרְדֳּכַ֣י אֶל־הַיְּהוּדִ֡ים וְאֶ֣ל הָאֲחַשְׁדַּרְפְּנִֽים־וְהַפַּחוֹת֩ וְשָׂרֵ֨י הַמְּדִינ֜וֹת אֲשֶׁ֣ר ׀ מֵהֹ֣דּוּ וְעַד־כּ֗וּשׁ שֶׁ֣בַע וְעֶשְׂרִ֤ים וּמֵאָה֙ מְדִינָ֔ה מְדִינָ֤ה וּמְדִינָה֙ כִּכְתָבָ֔הּ וְעַ֥ם וָעָ֖ם כִּלְשֹׁנ֑וֹ וְאֶ֨ל־הַיְּהוּדִ֔ים כִּכְתָבָ֖ם וְכִלְשׁוֹנָֽם: י וַיִּכְתֹּ֗ב בְּשֵׁם֙ הַמֶּ֣לֶךְ אֲחַשְׁוֵרֹ֔שׁ וַיַּחְתֹּ֖ם בְּטַבַּ֣עַת הַמֶּ֑לֶךְ וַיִּשְׁלַ֣ח סְפָרִ֡ים בְּיַד֩ הָרָצִ֨ים בַּסּוּסִ֜ים רֹכְבֵ֤י הָרֶ֨כֶשׁ֙ הָֽאֲחַשְׁתְּרָנִ֔ים בְּנֵ֖י הָֽרַמָּכִֽים:

יא אֲשֶׁר֩ נָתַ֨ן הַמֶּ֜לֶךְ לַיְּהוּדִ֣ים ׀ אֲשֶׁ֣ר ׀ בְּכָל־עִיר־וָעִ֗יר לְהִקָּהֵל֮ וְלַעֲמֹ֣ד עַל־נַפְשָׁם֒ לְהַשְׁמִיד֩ וְלַהֲרֹ֨ג וּלְאַבֵּ֜ד אֶת־כָּל־חֵ֣יל עַ֥ם וּמְדִינָ֛ה הַצָּרִ֥ים אֹתָ֖ם טַ֣ף וְנָשִׁ֑ים וּשְׁלָלָ֖ם לָבֽוֹז: יב בְּי֣וֹם אֶחָ֔ד בְּכָל־מְדִינ֖וֹת הַמֶּ֣לֶךְ אֲחַשְׁוֵר֑וֹשׁ בִּשְׁלוֹשָׁ֥ה עָשָׂ֛ר לְחֹ֥דֶשׁ שְׁנֵים־עָשָׂ֖ר הוּא־חֹ֥דֶשׁ אֲדָֽר:

11 The letter stated that the king gave permission to Jews in every city to join together and defend themselves. They could destroy and kill any army that wanted to hurt them — along with those people's wives and children. And the Jews were allowed to take those people's property.

12 They will be able to do this on one day, in every land ruled by King Achashveirosh; on the thirteenth day of the twelfth month which is the month of Adar.

A Closer Look

Verse 11 tells us that the Jews in every city could join together to beat their enemies. They joined together to pray to Hashem.

This teaches us a lesson: To truly make sure we can succeed against our enemies, we must gather together in prayer to Hashem.

13 The details of the law were announced in every country so that all the nations would know it, and so the Jews would be prepared to take revenge against all their enemies on that day.

14 The fast messengers, and the riders of the fast camels, left hurried and rushed according to the king's order. And in Shushan, the capital city, the law was announced.

יג פַּתְשֶׁגֶן הַכְּתָב לְהִנָּתֵן דָּת בְּכָל־מְדִינָה וּמְדִינָה גָּלוּי לְכָל־הָעַמֶּים וְלִהְיוֹת °הַיְּהוּדִים עֲתִידִים [°הַיְּהוּדִיים עתודים כ] לַיּוֹם הַזֶּה לְהִנָּקֵם מֵאֹיְבֵיהֶם: יד הָרָצִים רֹכְבֵי הָרֶכֶשׁ הָאֲחַשְׁתְּרָנִים יָצְאוּ מְבֹהָלִים וּדְחוּפִים בִּדְבַר הַמֶּלֶךְ וְהַדָּת נִתְּנָה בְּשׁוּשַׁן הַבִּירָה:

Did You Know??
The word מְבֹהָלִים, used in verse 14, can mean "rushed" but it can also mean "confused." This new letter was very surprising to the messengers. Throughout history, it was not unusual for a country to allow the Jews to be killed, but it was very unusual for a letter to be sent out saying that the Jews could and would defend themselves and destroy their enemies.

VERSES 15 AND 16 ARE EACH READ ALOUD FIRST BY THE CONGREGATION AND THEN BY THE READER.

¹⁵ Mordechai left the king's palace wearing royal clothing that was colored blue and white. He had a large gold crown, and a robe made of the finest linen and purple wool. And the city of Shushan rejoiced and was happy.

¹⁶ The Jews enjoyed light and happiness, joy and honor.

¹⁷ In every country, and in every city the king's letter reached, all the Jews were filled with joy and gladness. It was a time of feasting and a holiday. Many people tried to act Jewish, because they were now afraid of the Jews.

טו וּמָרְדֳּכַי יָצָא ׀ מִלִּפְנֵי הַמֶּלֶךְ בִּלְבוּשׁ מַלְכוּת תְּכֵלֶת וָחוּר וַעֲטֶרֶת זָהָב גְּדוֹלָה וְתַכְרִיךְ בּוּץ וְאַרְגָּמָן וְהָעִיר שׁוּשָׁן צָהֲלָה וְשָׂמֵחָה: טז לַיְּהוּדִים הָיְתָה אוֹרָה וְשִׂמְחָה וְשָׂשֹׂן וִיקָר:

יז וּבְכָל־מְדִינָה וּמְדִינָה וּבְכָל־עִיר וָעִיר מְקוֹם אֲשֶׁר דְּבַר־הַמֶּלֶךְ וְדָתוֹ מַגִּיעַ שִׂמְחָה וְשָׂשׂוֹן לַיְּהוּדִים מִשְׁתֶּה וְיוֹם טוֹב וְרַבִּים מֵעַמֵּי הָאָרֶץ מִתְיַהֲדִים כִּי־נָפַל פַּחַד־הַיְּהוּדִים עֲלֵיהֶם:

Did You Know??

Mordechai would not leave the king's palace until he was sure that the Jewish people was safe and secure. Only then did he leave the palace in his royal garments.

Verses 15 and 16 are each said out loud by the congregation and then repeated by the *chazan* reading the Megillah. Again, as in verse 2:5, we do this to publicize the miracle of Purim, and also as a sign of our joy over the miracles that happened to Mordechai and the Jewish people.

Chapter Nine — פרק ט

¹ And on the thirteenth day of the twelfth month, which is the month of Adar — the day the king's law took effect, the day on which the enemies of the Jews planned to defeat them — the exact opposite happened! The Jews defeated their enemies!

² The Jews gathered together in their cities, throughout the lands of King Achashverosh, to attack anyone who wanted to hurt them. No one stood up against the Jews, because all the nations were afraid of them.

א וּבִשְׁנֵים֩ עָשָׂ֨ר חֹ֜דֶשׁ הוּא־חֹ֣דֶשׁ אֲדָ֗ר בִּשְׁלוֹשָׁ֨ה עָשָׂ֥ר יוֹם֮ בּוֹ֒ אֲשֶׁ֣ר הִגִּ֣יעַ דְּבַר־הַמֶּ֛לֶךְ וְדָת֖וֹ לְהֵֽעָשׂ֑וֹת בַּיּ֗וֹם אֲשֶׁ֨ר שִׂבְּר֜וּ אֹיְבֵ֤י הַיְּהוּדִים֙ לִשְׁל֣וֹט בָּהֶ֔ם וְנַהֲפ֣וֹךְ ה֗וּא אֲשֶׁ֨ר יִשְׁלְט֧וּ הַיְּהוּדִ֛ים הֵ֖מָּה בְּשֹׂנְאֵיהֶֽם:

ב נִקְהֲל֣וּ הַיְּהוּדִ֗ים בְּעָרֵיהֶם֙ בְּכָל־מְדִינוֹת֙ הַמֶּ֣לֶךְ אֲחַשְׁוֵר֔וֹשׁ לִשְׁלֹ֣חַ יָ֔ד בִּמְבַקְשֵׁ֖י רָֽעָתָ֑ם וְאִישׁ֙ לֹא־עָמַ֣ד לִפְנֵיהֶ֔ם כִּֽי־נָפַ֥ל פַּחְדָּ֖ם עַל־כָּל־הָעַמִּֽים:

A Closer Look

Haman found that of the entire year, the 13th day of Adar was the one day that the Jews had no hope of being saved. Hashem showed how wrong he was!

A Closer Look

The thirteenth day of Adar finally arrived. Even though the king and his governors no longer supported killing the Jews, the descendants of Amalek tried to kill the Jews anyway because of their deep hatred towards the Jews.

The Jews fought their enemies and destroyed them.

³ And all the rulers of the countries, and the governors, and the governors, and everyone who worked for the king, respected the Jews because they were afraid of Mordechai.

⁴ Because Mordechai was important in the king's palace, and he became well known in every country, for he grew more and more important.

⁵ The Jews fought all their enemies, killing and destroying them with swords. They did as they pleased with their enemies.

גְוְכָל־שָׂרֵי הַמְּדִינוֹת וְהָאֲחַשְׁדַּרְפְּנִים וְהַפַּחוֹת וְעֹשֵׂי הַמְּלָאכָה אֲשֶׁר לַמֶּלֶךְ מְנַשְּׂאִים אֶת־הַיְּהוּדִים כִּי־נָפַל פַּחַד־מָרְדֳּכַי עֲלֵיהֶם: דכִּי־גָדוֹל מָרְדֳּכַי בְּבֵית הַמֶּלֶךְ וְשָׁמְעוֹ הוֹלֵךְ בְּכָל־הַמְּדִינוֹת כִּי־הָאִישׁ מָרְדֳּכַי הוֹלֵךְ וְגָדוֹל: הוַיַּכּוּ הַיְּהוּדִים בְּכָל־אֹיְבֵיהֶם מַכַּת־חֶרֶב וְהֶרֶג וְאַבְדָן וַיַּעֲשׂוּ בְשֹׂנְאֵיהֶם כִּרְצוֹנָם:

Did You Know??
At first the people thought that Mordechai was promoted because he once saved the king's life. Later they realized it was because he was really a great man.

Did You Know??
The Jews usually fasted and prayed when they went to war, just as Moshe Rabbeinu did when the Jews fought against Amalek. Today, the thirteenth day of Adar, the day the Jews fought against their enemies, as told in the Megillah, is a fast day called *Ta'anis Esther* — the Fast of Esther.

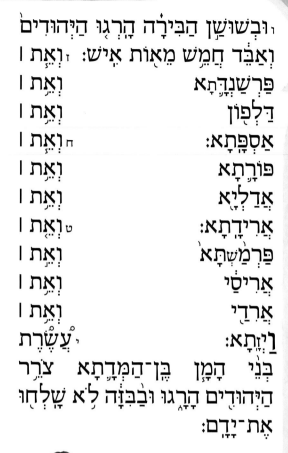

⁶ And in the capital Shushan, the Jews killed five hundred men. ⁷ And

Parshandasa,	and
Dalphon,	and
Aspasa,	⁸ and
Porasa,	and
Adalia,	and
Aridasa,	⁹ and
Parmashta,	and
Arisai,	and
Aridai,	and
Vayzasa,	¹⁰ the ten

sons of Haman, the son of Hamedasa, enemy of the Jewish people, they killed. But they did not take any of their property.

Did You Know??

When reading the Megillah, the names of Haman's ten sons are said in one breath. This is because they all died at the exact same moment.

Did You Know??

In the Megillah, the letter ו of the name וַיְזָתָא, Vayzasa, is very long and large, so it should be similar to a long pole. This is because all ten sons were hanged one above the other, on the very tall 50-cubit gallows that Haman had built.

A Closer Look

These five hundred people who were killed in Shushan were not simple people. They were important people, and all were descendants of Amalek!

A Closer Look

Mordechai had permitted the Jews to take the property of the people they killed. But the Jewish people themselves decided not to. They did not want anyone to think that they cared about other people's money.

A Closer Look

The poor people had the hardest time not taking the spoils because they were so needy. This is why the poor people receive *matanos l'evyonim* — gifts for the poor — every year on Purim.

[11] On that day, the king was told how many people were killed in Shushan, the capital city.

[12] The king said to Queen Esther:

"The Jewish people killed five hundred people in Shushan the capital city, and the ten sons of Haman. What they must have done in the rest of the king's countries! But what is your request? It will be given to you. What further do you want? It will be done."

[13] Esther said, "If it pleases the king, let the Jews who live in Shushan do tomorrow just as they did today. And let them hang Haman's ten sons on the gallows."

[14] The king commanded that this be done. The order was given in Shushan and they hanged the ten sons of Haman.

[15] So the Jews in Shushan also gathered together on the fourteenth day of the month of Adar, and they killed another three hundred men in Shushan. But they did not take any of the property.

יא בַּיּוֹם הַהוּא בָּא מִסְפַּר הַהֲרוּגִים בְּשׁוּשַׁן הַבִּירָה לִפְנֵי הַמֶּלֶךְ: יב וַיֹּאמֶר הַמֶּלֶךְ לְאֶסְתֵּר הַמַּלְכָּה בְּשׁוּשַׁן הַבִּירָה הָרְגוּ הַיְּהוּדִים וְאַבֵּד חֲמֵשׁ מֵאוֹת אִישׁ וְאֵת עֲשֶׂרֶת בְּנֵי־הָמָן בִּשְׁאָר מְדִינוֹת הַמֶּלֶךְ מֶה עָשׂוּ וּמַה־שְּׁאֵלָתֵךְ וְיִנָּתֵן לָךְ וּמַה־בַּקָּשָׁתֵךְ עוֹד וְתֵעָשׂ: יג וַתֹּאמֶר אֶסְתֵּר אִם־עַל־הַמֶּלֶךְ טוֹב יִנָּתֵן גַּם־מָחָר לַיְּהוּדִים אֲשֶׁר בְּשׁוּשָׁן לַעֲשׂוֹת כְּדָת הַיּוֹם וְאֵת עֲשֶׂרֶת בְּנֵי־הָמָן יִתְלוּ עַל־הָעֵץ: יד וַיֹּאמֶר הַמֶּלֶךְ לְהֵעָשׂוֹת כֵּן וַתִּנָּתֵן דָּת בְּשׁוּשָׁן וְאֵת עֲשֶׂרֶת בְּנֵי־הָמָן תָּלוּ: טו וַיִּקָּהֲלוּ °הַיְּהוּדִים [°הַיְּהוּדִים כ'] אֲשֶׁר־בְּשׁוּשָׁן גַּם בְּיוֹם אַרְבָּעָה עָשָׂר לְחֹדֶשׁ אֲדָר וַיַּהַרְגוּ בְשׁוּשָׁן שְׁלֹשׁ מֵאוֹת אִישׁ וּבַבִּזָּה לֹא שָׁלְחוּ אֶת־יָדָם:

Did You Know??
The only Jews who were allowed to fight their enemies on the fourteenth day of Adar were the Jews in Shushan.

A Closer Look
After the first day, the king was upset that so many Persians had been killed by the Jews. But an angel came and forced him to speak kindly to Esther.

A Closer Look
Haman's sons had been killed on the thirteenth day of Adar. Esther wanted their bodies to be hanged on the high pole becaause she wanted the people to see what happens to the enemies of the Jewish people.

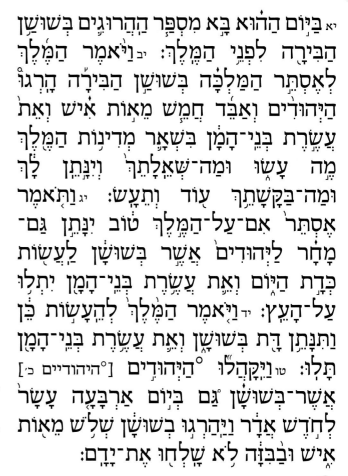

16 The rest of the Jews in the countries of the king gathered together and defended themselves. They rested from their enemies and killed seventy-five thousand of their foes. But they did not take anyone's property.

17 This happened on the thirteenth day of Adar. They rested on the fourteenth day, and made it a day of parties and happiness.

18 But the Jews who lived in Shushan gathered together on the thirteenth day of the month and on the fourteenth day, and they rested on the fifteenth day, making that day a day of parties and happiness.

19 This is why Jews who are spread out, who live in cities without walls, make the fourteenth day of Adar a day of happiness, parties, and a holiday, and of sending food to their friends.

טז וּשְׁאָר הַיְּהוּדִים אֲשֶׁר בִּמְדִינוֹת הַמֶּלֶךְ נִקְהֲלוּ וְעָמֹד עַל־נַפְשָׁם וְנוֹחַ מֵאֹיְבֵיהֶם וְהָרוֹג בְּשֹׂנְאֵיהֶם חֲמִשָּׁה וְשִׁבְעִים אָלֶף וּבַבִּזָּה לֹא שָׁלְחוּ אֶת־יָדָם: יז בְּיוֹם־שְׁלֹשָׁה עָשָׂר לְחֹדֶשׁ אֲדָר וְנוֹחַ בְּאַרְבָּעָה עָשָׂר בּוֹ וְעָשֹׂה אֹתוֹ יוֹם מִשְׁתֶּה וְשִׂמְחָה: יח וְהַיְּהוּדִים [°וְהַיְּהוּדִיִּים כ׳] אֲשֶׁר־בְּשׁוּשָׁן נִקְהֲלוּ בִּשְׁלֹשָׁה עָשָׂר בּוֹ וּבְאַרְבָּעָה עָשָׂר בּוֹ וְנוֹחַ בַּחֲמִשָּׁה עָשָׂר בּוֹ וְעָשֹׂה אֹתוֹ יוֹם מִשְׁתֶּה וְשִׂמְחָה: יט עַל־כֵּן הַיְּהוּדִים הַפְּרָזִים [°הַפְּרוֹזִים כ׳] הַיֹּשְׁבִים בְּעָרֵי הַפְּרָזוֹת עֹשִׂים אֵת יוֹם אַרְבָּעָה עָשָׂר לְחֹדֶשׁ אֲדָר שִׂמְחָה וּמִשְׁתֶּה וְיוֹם טוֹב וּמִשְׁלוֹחַ מָנוֹת אִישׁ לְרֵעֵהוּ:

Did You Know??

The Sanhedrin, led by Mordechai, established a festival on the day the Jews celebrated at the time of the miracle. Since the Jews throughout the empire celebrated on the 14th of Adar, Purim takes place on that day. In Shushan, however, the Jews celebrated on the 15th of Adar, so they made Purim in Shushan on the 15th. But they realized that Jews would not always be living in Shushan.

So they ruled that all cities like Shushan, that have a wall, would celebrate on the 15th of Adar. But they wanted to include Eretz Yisrael, which was in ruins at that time, in this honor, so they made a rule that any city that had a wall in the time of Yehoshua (which is when the Jews conquered Eretz Yisrael) would celebrate Purim on the 15th of Adar. The only city we are certain had a wall then is Jerusalem, where Purim is celebrated on Shushan Purim — the 15th of Adar.

²⁰ Mordechai wrote down these things that had happened. He sent letters out to all the Jews in all the countries that King Achashveirosh ruled, near and far.

²¹ He made a law that everyone should celebrate the fourteenth and fifteenth days of Adar every year.

²² These were the same dates that the Jews had rested from their enemies, and this was the month that was changed from worry to joy, from mourning to a holiday. These should be days of parties and happiness and sending gifts of food to their friends, and gifts for the poor.

²³ The Jewish people agreed to continue what they did then, and everything Mordechai wrote that they should do.

כ וַיִּכְתֹּב מָרְדֳּכַי אֶת־הַדְּבָרִים הָאֵלֶּה וַיִּשְׁלַח סְפָרִים אֶל־כָּל־הַיְּהוּדִים אֲשֶׁר בְּכָל־מְדִינוֹת הַמֶּלֶךְ אֲחַשְׁוֵרוֹשׁ הַקְּרוֹבִים וְהָרְחוֹקִים: כא לְקַיֵּם עֲלֵיהֶם לִהְיוֹת עֹשִׂים אֵת יוֹם אַרְבָּעָה עָשָׂר לְחֹדֶשׁ אֲדָר וְאֵת יוֹם־חֲמִשָּׁה עָשָׂר בּוֹ בְּכָל־שָׁנָה וְשָׁנָה: כב כַּיָּמִים אֲשֶׁר־נָחוּ בָהֶם הַיְּהוּדִים מֵאוֹיְבֵיהֶם וְהַחֹדֶשׁ אֲשֶׁר נֶהְפַּךְ לָהֶם מִיָּגוֹן לְשִׂמְחָה וּמֵאֵבֶל לְיוֹם טוֹב לַעֲשׂוֹת אוֹתָם יְמֵי מִשְׁתֶּה וְשִׂמְחָה וּמִשְׁלֹחַ מָנוֹת אִישׁ לְרֵעֵהוּ וּמַתָּנוֹת לָאֶבְיוֹנִים: כג וְקִבֵּל הַיְּהוּדִים אֵת אֲשֶׁר־הֵחֵלּוּ לַעֲשׂוֹת וְאֵת אֲשֶׁר־כָּתַב מָרְדֳּכַי אֲלֵיהֶם:

Did You Know??

To fulfill the *mitzvah* of *mishloach manos* — sending food to friends — we must send at least two foods to one person. *Matanos la'evyonim* — gifts for the poor — must be given to at least two poor people. The law is that on Purim we should give charity to anyone who asks, without checking if they really deserve it or not. Our Sages also teach us that it is better to spend more on giving to the poor than on sending food to friends.

²⁴ Because Haman the son of Hamedasa, the Agagite, enemy of all the Jewish people, planned to destroy the Jews; he made a *pur*, which is a lottery, to scare them and destroy them.

²⁵ But when Queen Esther came before the king, he ordered through letters that Haman's evil plan against the Jewish people be turned onto Haman's own head. And indeed, Haman and his sons were hanged on the gallows.

²⁶ This is why these days are called "Purim." It comes from the word "*pur*" — lottery. And because of all the things written in this letter — because of what caused them to do this, and everything that happened to them —

²⁷ the Jewish people accepted on themselves and on their descendants and on those who join them to celebrate, without fail, these two days, as it was written, at the proper time, every year.

²⁸ These days should be remembered and celebrated in every generation by every family, in every land, and in every city. The Jewish people will never stop celebrating these days of Purim, and they will always be remembered by their children.

כד כִּי הָמָן בֶּן־הַמְּדָ֫תָא הָאֲגָגִי צֹרֵר כָּל־הַיְּהוּדִים חָשַׁב עַל־הַיְּהוּדִים לְאַבְּדָם וְהִפִּל פּוּר הוּא הַגּוֹרָל לְהֻמָּם וּלְאַבְּדָם: כה וּבְבֹאָהּ לִפְנֵי הַמֶּ֫לֶךְ אָמַר עִם־הַסֵּפֶר יָשׁוּב מַחֲשַׁבְתּוֹ הָרָעָה אֲשֶׁר־חָשַׁב עַל־הַיְּהוּדִים עַל־רֹאשׁוֹ וְתָלוּ אֹתוֹ וְאֶת־בָּנָיו עַל־הָעֵץ: כו עַל־כֵּן קָרְאוּ לַיָּמִים הָאֵלֶּה פוּרִים עַל־שֵׁם הַפּוּר עַל־כֵּן עַל־כָּל־דִּבְרֵי הָאִגֶּרֶת הַזֹּאת וּמָה־רָאוּ עַל־כָּכָה וּמָה הִגִּיעַ אֲלֵיהֶם: כז קִיְּמוּ °וְקִבְּלוּ [°וְקִבֵּל כ] הַיְּהוּדִים ׀ עֲלֵיהֶם ׀ וְעַל־זַרְעָם וְעַל כָּל־הַנִּלְוִים עֲלֵיהֶם וְלֹא יַעֲבוֹר לִהְיוֹת עֹשִׂים אֵת־שְׁנֵי הַיָּמִים הָאֵלֶּה כִּכְתָבָם וְכִזְמַנָּם בְּכָל־שָׁנָה וְשָׁנָה: כח וְהַיָּמִים הָאֵלֶּה נִזְכָּרִים וְנַעֲשִׂים בְּכָל־דּוֹר וָדוֹר מִשְׁפָּחָה וּמִשְׁפָּחָה מְדִינָה וּמְדִינָה וְעִיר וָעִיר וִימֵי הַפּוּרִים הָאֵלֶּה לֹא יַעַבְרוּ מִתּוֹךְ הַיְּהוּדִים וְזִכְרָם לֹא־יָסוּף מִזַּרְעָם:

²⁹ Then Queen Esther — daughter of Avichail — and Mordechai the Jew wrote the greatness of the miracle to establish this second letter about Purim.

³⁰ Copies of this scroll were sent to all the Jews in the one hundred twenty-seven countries, the empire of Achashveirosh — words of peace and truth.

³¹ They were told to always keep these days of Purim on the correct dates, just as Mordechai the Jew and Queen Esther had told them to do, and the same way that they had accepted upon themselves and upon their children; a remembrance of the fasting and the prayers.

³² Esther asked that these words about Purim be accepted and that these events (written in the Megillah) be added to the *Tanach*.

כט וַתִּכְתֹּב אֶסְתֵּר הַמַּלְכָּה בַת־אֲבִיחַיִל וּמָרְדֳּכַי הַיְּהוּדִי אֶת־כָּל־תֹּקֶף לְקַיֵּם אֵת אִגֶּרֶת הַפֻּרִים הַזֹּאת הַשֵּׁנִית: ל וַיִּשְׁלַח סְפָרִים אֶל־כָּל־הַיְּהוּדִים אֶל־שֶׁבַע וְעֶשְׂרִים וּמֵאָה מְדִינָה מַלְכוּת אֲחַשְׁוֵרוֹשׁ דִּבְרֵי שָׁלוֹם וֶאֱמֶת: לא לְקַיֵּם אֶת־יְמֵי הַפֻּרִים הָאֵלֶּה בִּזְמַנֵּיהֶם כַּאֲשֶׁר קִיַּם עֲלֵיהֶם מָרְדֳּכַי הַיְּהוּדִי וְאֶסְתֵּר הַמַּלְכָּה וְכַאֲשֶׁר קִיְּמוּ עַל־נַפְשָׁם וְעַל־זַרְעָם דִּבְרֵי הַצּוֹמוֹת וְזַעֲקָתָם: לב וּמַאֲמַר אֶסְתֵּר קִיַּם דִּבְרֵי הַפֻּרִים הָאֵלֶּה וְנִכְתָּב בַּסֵּפֶר:

Did You Know??

The letter ת in the word וַתִּכְתֹּב — *wrote* — is written larger here. This teaches us that just as the ת is the last letter in the Hebrew alphabet, the Purim story is the last miracle included in the *Tanach* (the Bible).

A Closer Look

Mordechai wrote down everything that happened, and Esther explained how these events that seemed normal were all the work of Hashem. Who could have understood that the sins the Jews committed at Achashveirosh's party would lead to their near destruction nine years later? And who could have seen that after the Jewish people repented, Hashem would turn normal events around and bring a great salvation to the Jewish people?

Chapter Ten — פרק י

¹ **A**nd King Achashveirosh placed a tax throughout his entire country — on the mainland and the islands.

² All his great deeds and his power, and the spread of the greatness of Mordechai, whom the king had promoted, are written in the Book of the History of the Kings of Media and Persia.

אוַיָּשֶׂם֩ הַמֶּ֨לֶךְ °אֲחַשְׁוֵרֹ֧שׁ [°אחשרש כ'] ׀ מַ֛ס עַל־הָאָ֖רֶץ וְאִיֵּ֥י הַיָּֽם: בוְכָל־מַעֲשֵׂ֤ה תָקְפּוֹ֙ וּגְב֣וּרָת֔וֹ וּפָרָשַׁת֙ גְּדֻלַּ֣ת מָרְדֳּכַ֔י אֲשֶׁ֥ר גִּדְּל֖וֹ הַמֶּ֑לֶךְ הֲלוֹא־הֵ֣ם כְּתוּבִ֗ים עַל־סֵ֨פֶר֙ דִּבְרֵ֣י הַיָּמִ֔ים לְמַלְכֵ֖י מָדַ֥י וּפָרָֽס:

THE FINAL VERSE OF THE MEGILLAH IS READ ALOUD FIRST BY THE CONGREGATION AND THEN BY THE READER.

³ **For Mordechai the Jew was second in command to King Achashveirosh. Mordechai was great among the Jews, loved by most of them. He always tried to do good things for his people and to bring peace to all its children.**

גכִּ֣י ׀ מָרְדֳּכַ֣י הַיְּהוּדִ֗י מִשְׁנֶה֙ לַמֶּ֣לֶךְ אֲחַשְׁוֵר֔וֹשׁ וְגָדוֹל֙ לַיְּהוּדִ֔ים וְרָצ֖וּי לְרֹ֣ב אֶחָ֑יו דֹּרֵ֥שׁ טוֹב֙ לְעַמּ֔וֹ וְדֹבֵ֥ר שָׁל֖וֹם לְכָל־זַרְעֽוֹ:

> **Did You Know??**
>
> King Achashveirosh ruled Persia for only fourteen years. After he died, his son Darius II (Esther's son) took over as king. Darius II allowed the Jews to begin rebuilding the *Beis HaMikdash* in Jerusalem.

ברכה אחרי קריאת המגילה
Blessing After Reading the Megillah

After the *Megillah* reading, each member of the congregation recites the following blessing.
[This blessing is not recited unless a *minyan* is present for the reading.]

בָּרוּךְ אַתָּה יהוה אֱלֹהֵינוּ מֶלֶךְ הָעוֹלָם, (הָאֵל) הָרָב אֶת רִיבֵנוּ, וְהַדָּן אֶת דִּינֵנוּ, וְהַנּוֹקֵם אֶת נִקְמָתֵנוּ, וְהַמְשַׁלֵּם גְּמוּל לְכָל אֹיְבֵי נַפְשֵׁנוּ, וְהַנִּפְרָע לָנוּ מִצָּרֵינוּ. בָּרוּךְ אַתָּה יהוה, הַנִּפְרָע לְעַמּוֹ יִשְׂרָאֵל מִכָּל צָרֵיהֶם, הָאֵל הַמּוֹשִׁיעַ.

Blessed are You, HASHEM, our God, King of the universe, (the God) Who takes up our complaint, judges our claim, avenges our wrong; Who brings the right punishment upon all enemies of our soul and takes revenge for us from our foes. Blessed are You, HASHEM, Who takes revenge for His people Israel from all their foes, the God Who brings salvation.

We recite the following prayer at night after we finish reading the Megillah.
The entire story of Purim is retold here as a Hebrew poem.

אֲשֶׁר הֵנִיא עֲצַת גּוֹיִם, וַיָּפֶר מַחְשְׁבוֹת עֲרוּמִים. בְּקוּם עָלֵינוּ אָדָם רָשָׁע, נֵצֶר זָדוֹן, מִזֶּרַע עֲמָלֵק. גָּאָה בְעָשְׁרוֹ, וְכָרָה לוֹ בּוֹר, וּגְדֻלָּתוֹ יָקְשָׁה לּוֹ לָכֶד.

א He (Hashem) stopped the plot
of the nations,
and canceled the plans
of the cunning ones,

ב When an evil man (Haman)
stood up against us,
A descendent of evil (ones) —
an offspring of Amalek.

ג He boasted of his wealth,
and dug his own grave,
And his greatness
set the trap for him.

Did You Know ??
In this poem, each line begins with the next letter of the *alef-beis*.

ד He wanted to trap (the Jews), but he was trapped instead. He tried to wipe them out, but he was quickly wiped out.

ה Haman showed the hatred of his fathers, And he awakened the hatred of brothers (Esav's hatred for Yaakov) against the children,

ו And he (Haman) did not remember the mercy of King Shaul, Because it was through his mercy on Agag, that the enemy (Haman) was born.

ז The evil one (Haman) planned to kill the righteous one (Mordechai), But that impure person was trapped in the hands of the pure one.

ח His (Mordechai's) kindness was stronger than the error of his ancestor (Shaul), And the evil one (Haman) piled up sin upon his (Agag's) sins.

ט He (Haman) hid in his heart his scheming ideas, and dedicated himself to do evil.

י He tried to hurt Hashem's holy ones, And he gave his money (to the King) to cut off their memory.

כ When Mordechai saw that (Hashem's) anger had come forth, And Haman's laws were announced in Shushan,

דִּמָּה בְנַפְשׁוֹ לִלְכֹּד, וְנִלְכַּד,
בִּקֵשׁ לְהַשְׁמִיד, וְנִשְׁמַד מְהֵרָה.
הָמָן הוֹדִיעַ אֵיבַת אֲבוֹתָיו,
וְעוֹרֵר שִׂנְאַת אַחִים לַבָּנִים.
וְלֹא זָכַר רַחֲמֵי שָׁאוּל,
כִּי בְחֶמְלָתוֹ עַל אֲגָג נוֹלַד אוֹיֵב.

Did You Know??

Hashem commanded King Shaul to destroy the nation of Amalek. He was supposed to wipe out all their men, women, children and even their animals. Saul did not listen to Hashem, and took pity on their king, Agag and let him live, and this is how he had a great-grandson, Haman who tried to destroy the Jews. If Shaul had done the right thing, Haman would never have been born.

זָמַם רָשָׁע לְהַכְרִית צַדִּיק,
וְנִלְכַּד טָמֵא, בִּידֵי טָהוֹר.
חֶסֶד גָּבַר עַל שִׁגְגַת אָב,
וְרָשָׁע הוֹסִיף חֵטְא עַל חֲטָאָיו.
טָמַן בְּלִבּוֹ מַחְשְׁבוֹת עֲרוּמָיו,
וַיִּתְמַכֵּר לַעֲשׂוֹת רָעָה.
יָדוֹ שָׁלַח בִּקְדוֹשֵׁי אֵל,
כַּסְפּוֹ נָתַן לְהַכְרִית זִכְרָם.
כִּרְאוֹת מָרְדְּכַי, כִּי יָצָא קֶצֶף,
וְדָתֵי הָמָן נִתְּנוּ בְשׁוּשָׁן.

ל He dressed himself in sackcloth
and went into mourning,
He decreed a fast and he sat in ashes.

מ "Who can come to atone
for our errors,
And (make Hashem) forgive
the sins of our ancestors?"

נ A flower grew out of a date tree,
Hadassah (Esther) arose
to awaken the sleeping Jews

ס Her servants rushed Haman
(to the banquet),
To make him drink the wine
that became his poison.

ע He stood with his riches,
but fell with his wickedness,
He made a gallows,
and was himself hung from it.

פ All the people of the world
opened their mouths
(to praise Hashem),
because the lot of Haman
changed into our Purim festival.

צ The tzaddik (Mordechai) was saved
from the wicked man (Haman),
The enemy (Haman) was
given (the gallows),
instead of him (Mordechai)

ק They (the Jews) accepted upon
themselves to celebrate Purim,
To rejoice every year.

ר You (Hashem) saw the prayers
of Mordechai and Esther,
Haman and his sons You hung
from the gallows.

לָבַשׁ שַׂק וְקָשַׁר מִסְפֵּד,
וְגָזַר צוֹם, וַיֵּשֶׁב עַל הָאֵפֶר.

מִי זֶה יַעֲמֹד לְכַפֵּר שְׁגָגָה,
וְלִמְחֹל חַטַּאת עֲוֹן אֲבוֹתֵינוּ.

נֵץ פָּרַח מִלּוּלָב,
הֵן הֲדַסָּה עָמְדָה
לְעוֹרֵר יְשֵׁנִים.

A Closer Look
In Hebrew a date palm is called
a *lulav*. Succos, it is held together
with an *esrog* (a citron), a *hadas* (a
myrtle) and an *aravah* (a willow). Esther's name
was also Haddasah, so this verse compares her
to a flower "growing from" *lulav*.

סָרִיסֶיהָ הִבְהִילוּ לְהָמָן,
לְהַשְׁקוֹתוֹ יֵין חֲמַת תַּנִּינִים.

עָמַד בְּעָשְׁרוֹ, וְנָפַל בְּרִשְׁעוֹ,
עָשָׂה לוֹ עֵץ, וְנִתְלָה עָלָיו.

פִּיהֶם פָּתְחוּ, כָּל יוֹשְׁבֵי תֵבֵל,
כִּי פוּר הָמָן נֶהְפַּךְ לְפוּרֵנוּ.

צַדִּיק נֶחֱלַץ מִיַּד רָשָׁע,
אוֹיֵב נִתַּן תַּחַת נַפְשׁוֹ.

קִיְּמוּ עֲלֵיהֶם, לַעֲשׂוֹת פּוּרִים,
וְלִשְׂמֹחַ בְּכָל שָׁנָה וְשָׁנָה.

רָאִיתָ אֶת תְּפִלַּת מָרְדֳּכַי וְאֶסְתֵּר,
הָמָן וּבָנָיו עַל הָעֵץ תָּלִיתָ.

We recite **Shoshanas Yaakov** after reading the Megillah both at night and in the morning. In many places it is sung with a happy tune.

ש The rose of Yaakov
(the Jewish People)
rejoiced and was happy,
when together they saw
Mordechai dressed
in his royal clothing.

ת You (Hashem) are always the
One to save the Jewish People,
You are their hope
in every generation.

To let people know that
those who hope for Your help
will not be ashamed,
And that all who rely on You
will never be embarrassed.

Cursed is Haman,
who tried to destroy me,
Blessed is Mordechai, the Jew.

Cursed is Zeresh, the wife of
the man who frightened me,
Blessed is Esther,
who helped me,
And also Charvonah
should be remembered for good.

שׁוֹשַׁנַּת יַעֲקֹב
צָהֲלָה וְשָׂמֵחָה,
בִּרְאוֹתָם יַחַד
תְּכֵלֶת מָרְדְּכָי.
תְּשׁוּעָתָם הָיִיתָ לָנֶצַח,
וְתִקְוָתָם בְּכָל דּוֹר וָדוֹר.

לְהוֹדִיעַ,
שֶׁכָּל קֹוֶיךָ לֹא יֵבשׁוּ,
וְלֹא יִכָּלְמוּ לָנֶצַח
כָּל הַחוֹסִים בָּךְ.

אָרוּר הָמָן,
אֲשֶׁר בִּקֵּשׁ לְאַבְּדִי,
בָּרוּךְ מָרְדְּכַי הַיְּהוּדִי.
אֲרוּרָה זֶרֶשׁ, אֵשֶׁת מַפְחִידִי,
בְּרוּכָה אֶסְתֵּר בַּעֲדִי,
וְגַם חַרְבוֹנָה זָכוּר לַטּוֹב.

A Closer Look

The prayer שׁוֹשַׁנַּת יַעֲקֹב is a continuation of אֲשֶׁר הֵנִיא. The last line there starts with the letter ר. The prayer שׁוֹשַׁנַּת יַעֲקֹב starts with the letter שׁ, and the next verse (תְּשׁוּעָתָם) starts with the letter ת, the last letter of the Hebrew alphabet.

Did You Know??

The Jewish People are compared to a rose. A rose is beautiful and sweet smelling, but surrounded by thorns. The Jewish People are also beautiful and sweet smelling, but are often surrounded by thorns — wicked nations.

Selected Laws of Purim

1. Purim is celebrated on the fourteenth day of Adar. Our Sages teach us that the month of Adar is a month of joy for the Jewish people.

A Closer Look

King Achashveirosh ruled over the whole world. With the king's permission, the wicked Haman planned to kill all the Jews on the thirteenth day of Adar. But Mordechai, the leader of the Jews, and his cousin Esther, queen of Persia, instructed the people to do *teshuvah* and pray to Hashem. Esther convinced Achashveirosh to let the Jews live. Haman, his sons, and the enemies of the Jews were killed instead. This miracle is celebrated on Purim.

2. The thirteenth day of Adar is a fast day. It is called *Ta'anis Esther*.

Did You Know??

Instead of being killed, the Jews were allowed to kill their enemies on the thirteenth day of Adar. They celebrated their victory on the fourteenth day, which is now the holiday called Purim. In Shushan, the capital city, the Jews were also allowed to kill their enemies on the fourteenth day of Adar. Therefore, they celebrated on the fifteenth day of Adar, which is called Shushan Purim.

Our Sages made a rule that all cities that were — like Shushan — surrounded by a wall, should celebrate Purim on the fifteenth of Adar. But at that time, *Eretz Yisrael* was in ruins, and our Sages didn't want Jerusalem to be thought of as an unimportant city. So they decided that any city that had a wall in the time of Yehoshua (which is when the Jews conquered *Eretz Yisrael* many years earlier) would celebrate Purim on the fifteenth day of Adar, just like Shushan. Jerusalem is the only city that we know for sure had a wall then, and Purim there is celebrated on Shushan Purim — the fifteenth of Adar.

Did You Know??

The Jewish people fasted on the day when they fought their enemies.

Also, Queen Esther asked them to fast and pray for three days and nights before she went to speak to King Achashveirosh. Even though that fast was not in Adar (it was actually in the month of Nissan), we fast just before Purim, the holiday that celebrates the miracle tof Purim.

3. On Purim, Megillas Esther is read, from a scroll of parchment. This is done at night and again in the morning.

A Closer Look

Every man and woman must hear the reading of the Megillah both on Purim night and on Purim morning. We must hear every single word of the Megillah. In many places, the person reading the Megillah repeats the name of Haman after the people stop making noise, to make sure that everyone hears the name being read from the scroll. It is best to hear the Megillah in shul with a *minyan*.

4. Before Purim begins, it is customary to give a half-dollar to charity. This is called *machatzis hashekel*.

5. On Purim we add the prayer "*Al HaNissim*" when we say the *Shemoneh Esrei* and *Birkas HaMazon*.

Did You Know??

The Megillah tells the story of Purim. When people hear the name Haman, they make noise or stamp their feet to "wipe out" his name. Haman came from Amalek, the nation that is the eternal enemy of the Jewish people.

Hashem's Name is not mentioned in the Megillah. This teaches us that even when we do not see how Hashem is helping us, we should know that He is still guiding everything that happens.

The person reading the Megillah recites the names of Haman's ten sons in one breath. This is because they were all hanged at the same time.

Did You Know??

This half-dollar reminds us of the half-shekel that was given in the time of the *Beis HaMikdash,* during the month of Adar, for buying public sacrifices.

The custom is to give three half-dollars.

People give half of whichever kind of money is used in their country. Depending on where they live, they will give either a half-dollar, a half-pound, a half-shekel, or a half-ruble.

Did You Know??

Al HaNissim tells us about the miracle of Purim — how Haman tried to destroy the Jewish people, but Hashem saved us and destroyed Haman and his sons instead.